WHAT ABIGAIL DID THAT SUMMER

By Ben Aaronovitch:

Rivers of London novels

Rivers of London
Moon Over Soho
Whispers Under Ground
Broken Homes
Foxglove Summer
The Hanging Tree
Lies Sleeping
False Value

Rivers of London novellas

The Furthest Station
The October Man

Rivers of London graphic novels

Body Work
Night Witch
Black Mould
Cry Fox
Water Weed
Action at a Distance
The Fey and the Furious

WHAT ABIGAIL DID THAT SUMMER

BEN AARONOVITCH

First published in Great Britain in 2021 by Gollancz
an imprint of The Orion Publishing Group Ltd
Carmelite House, 50 Victoria Embankment
London EC4Y 0DZ

An Hachette UK Company

1 3 5 7 9 10 8 6 4 2

Copyright © Ben Aaronovitch 2021

The moral right of Ben Aaronovitch to be identified as
the author of this work has been asserted in accordance
with the Copyright, Designs and Patents Act of 1988.

A CIP catalogue record for this book is
available from the British Library.

ISBN (Hardback) 978 1 473 22434 6
ISBN (eBook) 978 1 473 22436 0

Typeset by Input Data Services Ltd, Somerset

Printed and bound in Great Britain by Clays Ltd, Elcograf S.p.A.

This book is dedicated to all the
essential workers everywhere.

THE COURT OF THE
GODDESS OF THE FLEET

KENWOOD LADIES
BATHING POND

PARLIAMENT
HILL

HIGHGATE
NUMBER 1 POND
(WHERE I SACRIFICED
MY PHONE)

KITE HILL

WHERE I
MET SIMON

TO MY
ENDS

GOSPEL OAK STATION
(AKA FOX HQ)

Все счастливые семьи похожи друг на друга, каждая несчастливая семья несчастлива по-своему.

All happy families are alike; each unhappy family is unhappy in its own way.

Leo Tolstoy, *Anna Karenina*

Oh Bondage Up Yours!

Marianne Joan Elliott-Said (Poly Styrene)

1

Achieving Best Evidence

'm sitting in an interview room in Holmes Road police station. It's not like the ones you see on TV, with bare walls, a table and an old-fashioned twin-deck tape recorder. Who makes those machines anyway, and where are they getting the cassette tapes from? Somebody somewhere is making a ton of cash selling obsolete gear to the Metropolitan Police.

Anyway, the room I'm in has low-slung wood seating with foam cushions covered in pastel-coloured fabric. There is an open space with a red and yellow rug and beanbag seats. Against the wall are shelves with the sort of board games and cheap plastic toys you can buy down the market or in Poundland.

The room also has a pair of perspex domes fixed to the ceiling where the CCTV cameras hide, and somewhere nearby will be a room with monitors and recorders and probably a senior police officer of detective inspector rank or higher. I know the Feds. I know how they work. And I know that this is the Achieving Best Evidence suite, ABE, where they interview children and victims of sexual assault.

Or catch a crafty nap on night shift, Peter says. But Peter isn't here right now. He's in Herefordshire, hunting his own set of missing kids.

A white woman enters, a typical Fed with an off-the-peg suit, a lying face and suspicious eyes. She says her name is Kay but the name on the warrant card hanging on a lanyard around her neck is Karen Jonquiere. She will be an experienced detective constable with special training in interviewing traumatised children and stroppy teens. This is why she's stressing her northern accent – going for that no-nonsense *Coronation Street* mood. She's impatient, unconsciously tapping her foot. There are missing kids, time is of the essence. Deep down, I know, she wants to grab me and shake me until I tell her what she wants to know. I get that a lot. But the last adult that got physical with me ended up barred from working with children – and that's after he got out of hospital.

She knows all this, of course. She's read my file, which means she knows about the Folly and about the magic. But she's the type that won't believe in the supernatural until it pops up and slaps her in the face.

She glances down at the untouched plate of biscuits and the drink that sits between us on the coffee table.

'You're not hungry?' she asks.

I'm actually bare hungry and my stomach is growling. But I like being hungry sometimes. I like the feeling of being in control of my own body, my own wants and needs. I'm not anorexic, right? That's important. When I look in the mirror I see myself the way I am. It's good discipline not to give in, not to just grab the first tasty thing that comes your way. I'm thirsty, too. But the drink they brought me was easier to resist – I mean, Capri-Sun. What were they thinking?

Hungry and thirsty makes me keen, makes me sharp

like a knife. Because whatever Lady Fed thinks, I ain't here to answer questions. Quite the contrary, really.

'Who's still missing?' I ask.

Lady Fed's eyes narrow but she says nothing.

'Did Jessica come home?' I ask, and there is a tiny reaction. A tightening of the lips.

Yeah, I think, Jessica just walked out, didn't she? Turned up at her yard as if nothing happened and her mum hadn't been sticking photos of her on every lamp-post from Chalk Farm to Tufnell Park. Some of the kids wandered in and out like the house was a youth centre and they were doing a summer activities course. Some people got to stay. These would be the ones Lady Fed was interested in.

'What about Natali?' I ask, and Lady Fed is frowning because she so wants to ask who's Natali, but can't because I've got to have an appropriate adult because I'm thirteen – that's the law, that is.

I could name other names but you don't want to push the Feds too far. They can get obstreperous and this one's already giving me the squinty-eyed look that adults always give me after meeting me for more than five minutes.

'We're trying to help here, you know,' she says.

To keep her sweet I pick up the Capri-Sun, strip out the straw and punch it into the juice pouch. I take a long pull, which calms Lady Fed down a bit and gives me time to think. Obviously some of the children are leaking out of the house and some are not – what the differences are between them might be the clue I'm looking for.

The door opens and Simon's mum walks in.

She is one of them big little white women who spends

3

her days ordering men around a conference table, and her evenings making plans for Nigel or Tarquin or Fionnuala or whatever their kids are called. She was obviously off duty when the police called her, because she's wearing navy trousers and a beige cashmere roll-neck jumper. A couple of kids at my school have mums like her, or at least the trendy *Let's send our kids to the local comprehensive to show how right-on we are* versions.

Simon's mum isn't right-on or trendy, but I reckon she's my best chance of walking out of the fuzz box without so much as a social worker's report.

Whoever Lady Fed was expecting to turn up, it wasn't Simon's mum, who is now showing her a laminated photo ID which she slips back into her jacket before I can get a good look.

Lady Fed is made of sterner stuff, because she holds up a hand to stop Simon's mum in her tracks and turns to me.

'This woman cannot be your appropriate adult,' she says.

'Why not?' I ask.

'Because it would be inappropriate,' she says.

'Why's that, then?' I ask.

Lady Fed mentally reviews her answers and realises that she doesn't have an objection she can say out loud. So she smoothly changes tack, which is well slick and I get a better opinion of her.

'Don't you think one of your parents would be more suitable?' she asks.

I look at Simon's mum again – her face is a total mask. It's actually kind of cool how mask-like her face is. I wish I could do a face like that. Like not all the time, right?

But just when I need it. You know. On special occasions.

'She is suitable,' I say. 'A responsible person aged eighteen or over who is not a police officer or a person employed by the police.'

As set out in Section 38 (4)(a) Crime and Disorder Act 1998 – but I've learnt the hard way not to quote statutes at the Feds. They don't like it and it makes them suspicious.

Lady Fed shrugs and turns to Simon's mum.

'She's all yours,' she says.

Simon's mum settles in the chair beside me. The detective opens her mouth but before she can speak Simon's mum turns on me and, baring her teeth, snarls.

'You little wretch,' she says. 'Where's my son?'

2

The Lost Boy

'Hello,' he says. 'What's your name?'

'He' is a good-looking white boy, taller than me but about my age. Dark brown hair, big face, blue eyes under long lashes. He's dressed in a pair of cargo shorts and a bright red polo shirt. He looks like he should smell of shampoo and money.

I give him the look, but he just waits patiently for me to answer.

This vexes me – the look usually works – but it also makes me curious.

'What's your name?' I ask.

He smiles, showing perfect white teeth.

'Simon,' he says.

We are standing at the entrance to Hampstead Heath at the point where Parliament Hill Road ends. Despite it being morning, the heat has bleached the colour out of the air and made my scalp dry and itchy under my Rasta hat.

I tell Simon my name and he says it back to me as if I'm a teacher and we're in class.

'Abigail,' he says. 'Pleased to meet you.'

I deliberately don't respond but he's just gazing at me expectantly as if he's waiting for instructions. It's bare

6

creepy but also interesting. I know if I walk away the mystery's going to vex me forever.

I look around to see if maybe there's an appropriate adult nearby, a nanny maybe, chatting on their mobile now she's away from the mother and not paying attention. But there's no one obviously nanny-ish around, and anyway Simon is too old to need one.

A skinny white woman jogs past us in a pair of red short shorts and a yellow Lycra top, her legs bending awkwardly inwards as she goes. Following her is a dachshund, wheezing in the heat as it tries to keep up. We both watch the poor dog go past.

'That lady needs a bigger dog,' says Simon.

'Or maybe pull it along on a trolley,' I say.

'Dog on a skateboard,' says Simon, and just like that we're friends.

For the day at least.

'Were you waiting for someone?' I ask.

'Jessica,' he says and smiles, which then fades into a frown. 'But she didn't come.'

Now this is interesting to me, because I was supposed to meet someone in the same spot. A girl from my old primary school called Natali, who I hadn't seen for ages but suddenly turned up round my flats. Which is weird since I didn't think she knew anyone from my ends. Her mum and dad were both media types and had got her into Marylebone when I went to Burghley. She ran over and hugged me when she saw me and asked to come in for tea, but Paul was being a bit rowdy just then so we ended up in a café instead. Natali paid, which normally I mind, but to be honest I was too glad to be out of the flat to object.

'We're having an event,' she said.

'What kind of an event?' I asked.

'A happening,' she said, and before I could point out that a 'happening' was just a synonym for 'event' and just as short of actual information, she explained. They was going to have a 'happening' on Hampstead Heath, all kids from the area with food, drink, dancing, billiards, music and dressing up.

'And dancing,' said Natali once more for emphasis, which just showed she didn't really remember me that well. After she'd given me the time and place of the 'happening' and cut, I stayed in the café and made some notes in my Falcon diary. Peter gave me my first one because he knew that getting me involved in magic was the only way to keep me out of trouble. This one was diary number three, but only because I write small.

Natali had been talking in a weird sing-song voice, which was causing all sorts of proximity warnings to go off in my head. Now, maybe going to posh school makes you talk like you're guesting on *Tikkabilla*,* but I thought it was worth a bit of investigation. Something I could show Peter when he got back from the middle of nowhere. Me and Simon are standing where we're supposed to be, but no Natali and no Jessica. And def no 'happening' happening. Given we've been there ages, I'm wondering if I should wait longer to see if anybody else turns up.

* Notes for Agent Reynolds by Harold Postmartin, MA, DPhil (Oxon), FRS, AFSW – Thomas has asked me to provide a few explanatory notes. In this case, *Tikkabilla* is the name of a children's television programme, although the allusion to the presenter's voice escapes me as well.

Simon is still smiling and seems content to wait for-ever. I'm not, but Natali never gave me her number so I can't text or nothing.

'I was supposed to meet someone here too,' I say to fill the void.

Simon nods.

'Are they here?' he asks.

I say that I don't think they're coming.

'Would you like to see something interesting?' asks Simon.

'Okay,' I say, and Simon just turns and walks away up the path. Heading further onto the Heath. I consider letting him go but curiosity makes me follow.

'Where are we going?' I ask as I catch up.

'To see the Cat Lady,' says Simon.

3

The Cat Lady

I hate it when people ask me stupid questions. You're chatting about something and they say something like, 'Photosynthesis? What's that?' with that stupid look on their face like they is proud of their ignorance or something. I'm thinking, you've got a phone, right? Look it up. But if you say that, they just tell you they can't be bothered because, 'Photosynthesis? If it was important, right, there'd be an app.' So I don't say that.

And I don't tell them what chlorophyll does either, because that would be a waste of my time.

Hampstead Heath is a heath, from the old English *hæth* meaning wasteland, because it consists of a big sandy ridge that stretches across the top of Camden. The sand makes the soils acidic, which meant nobody ploughed it for crops and it was only good for sporadic grazing, sand extraction and large-scale landscape gardening.

Sir Thomas 'Wasteman' Maryon tried to build a big housing estate on it but there was a public protest and he was stopped. But not before he built a totally fake red brick 'viaduct' across a pond which now gives its name to the path that runs from the barrows to Whitestone Pond at the top of the hill.

Finding all that out took me five minutes on my phone while I was standing on the actual viaduct in the dark this March. And I was looking for ghosts, all right, but all I found were some olds looking for a quick hook-up after work before catching the bus home.

We're running across the viaduct now because Simon seems to run everywhere. The slowest he goes is a quick trot, as if he's missing his lower gears and only has two speeds. The creepy still one and the fast one.

I can keep up but I wouldn't want to do this all day.

I see I'm going to have to teach him how to walk proper. What Peter, who is a Fed, calls proceeding.

If you run everywhere you miss stuff that you might have been better off noticing – just saying.

We run up the viaduct path until we're up by the second fairground site.

Simon is pointing down into the valley between the path and Heath Street. It's full of trees and bushes.

'Down there,' he says.

'Down there what?'

'Down there lives the Cat Lady,' he says, and runs down the grass slope towards the trees.

Fortunately we're not in the real countryside so there's lots of paths and no chance of being eaten by yokels. Simon seems to know where he's going and is leading me to a particular rhododendron bush. He crouches down and crawls inside and I follow.

We are inside a hollow inside the bush. The space is cramped and hot with both of us in there. I can smell the flowers and the earth and a sharp smell that I realise is coming from Simon. It's not horrible or anything, but it seems strange to be close enough to smell him like this. His bare arm is right by my face and I've got this mad urge to lick the smooth pale skin of his biceps to see what he tastes like – which freaks me out, so I say something instead.

'I can't see anything,' I whisper.

Simon shushes me and points.

I shuffle forward until I can see through the leaves. Ahead of me is a clearing under the spreading canopy of a mature oak tree. There is a short stretch of grass with a park bench at one end. On the bench sits an old white lady.

She dresses like she's homeless, in a great big green army coat that is too big for her and too hot for summer. Her hair is grey and long, really long, hanging down over her face and shoulders. She has little round glasses and black fingerless gloves. On one side of her is a shopping trolley made of worn blue canvas, and with wheels that I'm sure are too big to be standard, with the kind of tyre tread you're more likely to see on a mountain bike. On the other side is a cardboard box the size of a bread bin.

The old lady is smacking her lips together and making a growling cough noise in the back of her throat. I'm thinking that maybe she's wandered off from a care home and that maybe we should be backing away slowly – for her sake if not for ours – when I sense something magical.

I know wizards, real wizards, who do real magic, and they've been teaching me to recognise magic when it happens in front of me. They call the sensations *vestigia* because they're old-fashioned and put Latin on everything. You have to know what you're looking for if you want to spot it.

So behind the lip smacking and coughing and growling, I can sense that off meat smell that tinned cat food has. Sense because it's not a real smell, it's just something that manifests itself in your mind as a smell.

The first cat arrives quickly, a battered black and white tom with a missing ear. It slinks up to the old lady and starts stroking itself against her foot. She ignores it and carries on making her noises. Two more cats arrive from different directions, a ginger and a tortoiseshell, then a fluffy white thing that looks far too clean to be sleeping rough. Then a tiger-striped moggie, followed by a very small Siamese which is limping on its left front leg.

The Cat Lady reaches into her shopping trolley and brings out a stack of plastic food containers and rips the tops off. I get a real whiff of cat food this time and wonder if I was wrong about the *vestigia*. That's the problem with magic, it takes practice to separate it from the everyday noise inside your head.

And my head can get pretty noisy sometimes.

The cats are falling upon the food, as they do, and the Cat Lady reaches out and grabs the big tom by the scruff of its neck and lifts it in front of her face. She peers at it, turning it this way and that, still making her weird noises.

The cat hangs limply and – although I can't really see from where I am and, of course, it's a cat – it looks *bored*. As if it's willing to hang a bit for some free food.

The Cat Lady puts the tom down, which cuffs one of its fellow felines out of the way and claims a food container to itself. The Cat Lady reaches down and picks up the tortoiseshell one. This one is hissing and clawing – I see a scratch appear on the sleeve of the lady's coat and another, red and glistening, on her hand. She doesn't flinch but keeps peering short-sightedly at the cat squirming in her grasp.

Then she is putting down the tortoiseshell and picking up the next cat – the Siamese with the limp. This one is different because the Cat Lady is reaching out with her other hand to touch the injured leg. The cat mewls and twists as she grasps its paw and manipulates it like my dad buying mangoes in Ridley Road.

The Cat Lady is nodding to herself and smacking her lips as she drops the little Siamese into the open neck of her shopping trolley.

I'm tensing because I don't like the look of this. I'm not in love with cats but I don't hold with unnecessary animal cruelty. One part of me is thinking that she's an old lady and it wouldn't be hard to liberate the cat, but another part of me, the part that knows magic is real, is thinking that some olds aren't really what they look like. You don't want to start a beef with something until you know what it is – that's just common sense, isn't it?

So I hold off and a few minutes later the old lady opens the cardboard box on the bench beside her and pulls out a scruffy black and white cat with a bandage around its hind leg. She holds it up by the scruff and checks the leg – which gets her a grumpy look and a whine. She gently places it in amongst its fellow cats who, still nomming up the cat food, pay it no attention.

'She feeds them,' says Simon as we walk back down the viaduct path. We're not jogging but that's probably only because there was an ice cream van at Whitestone Pond and we each got a 99. 'And she takes the sick ones to cat hospital.'

Simon says he's been watching the Cat Lady all summer but hasn't told anybody until he told me.

'Mum says that feeding stray cats should be against the law,' says Simon.

'Only if it constitutes a public nuisance,' I say, which I don't know if that's actually true but for some reason I want to sound clever in front of Simon.

'Should we tell the police?' he asks.

'Nah,' I say. 'Feds got better things to do.'

4

Feds at the Gate

And, speak of the devil, there's Feds waiting for us at the Parliament Hill Road gate, although actually they don't know they're waiting for us and we ain't about to tell them. There's two of them, a man and a woman, both white, both sweaty and red-faced in their uniforms. I don't want to be unfair, but the man really wanted to let his stab vest out a bit around the middle because he didn't look comfortable at all. They're both wearing the same professionally friendly smiles that Feds have when they do school visits.

The female Fed is writing something on a clipboard but the male Fed is tracking us like he was a radar.

'Hello,' he says, and waves at us.

I try to keep walking but the man strides over to stand in our way.

'I wonder if I might ask you a few questions,' he says.

'Are we in trouble?' asks Simon.

'No, not at all,' says the female Fed as she joins us. 'We just want to ask you a few questions.'

'What about?' I ask, and both the Feds narrow their eyes at me.

'Have you heard about the missing girls?' asks the male Fed.

'The ones in the village?' asks Simon.

The Feds are looking puzzled, so I help them out because I'm public-spirited that way.

'Rushpool,' I say.

Which is where Peter is, and not here running interference for me like he should be.

'Local girls,' says the male Fed, and me and Simon solemnly shake our heads even though I've got a bad feeling about this. Confirmed when the female Fed flips some pages on her clipboard and shows me a picture of Natali.

I shake my head again and she flips the page to show another white girl, about my age, with blonde hair and a pointy nose and chin.

'Jessica,' says Simon.

The female Fed is all interest now.

'Do you know her?' she asks.

Simon says nothing, but tilts his head to the side as if thinking about it.

The male Fed opens his mouth to speak, but Simon says, 'No, not really.'

But that never works with the Feds, which is why I said nothing. If you admit to anything they've always got more questions like, 'When did you last see her?' Which is what they ask him.

'Yesterday,' says Simon, and that leads to where and when, and what were you doing, and are you sure that was the last time you saw her, and was she your girl-friend? That last question makes Simon blush so hard he goes bright pink – I've never seen a real person go that colour before.

The Feds are not happy with his answers which consist

of, 'here', 'yesterday', 'playing', and 'definitely because I went home for tea' and 'No!' But this is a canvass, what they call door-to-door, and they can't get intense with kids without making it formal and that means getting an appropriate adult. They ask our names and addresses – they always ask for them.

I give him the surname of a different Abigail that I know is my age, goes to La Sainte Union and lives off Chetwynd Road. The female Fed nods and writes it down on her clipboard. Simon says his surname is Fletcher and gives an address in Belsize Park. Then, because Simon doesn't seem to be planning to leave, I grab his hand and lead him away down Parliament Hill.

'Is that really your surname?' asks Simon as we leave the Feds behind.

I tell him it isn't and he wants to know why I lied.

I explain about how when they get back to the cop shop the Feds are going to enter our names and our statements into a big computer program called HOLMES 2, where we will become nominals and stay there forever or until the case is closed. It's a magical thing, I tell him, but once the Feds have your name they start to attach random facts to it and those facts link up and the next thing you know, nice Mr Fed is knocking on your door and asking to see your mother because of something that happened ages ago and in any case the car was barely damaged at all and you shouldn't be driving a 4×4 around in central London anyway.

I leave out the bit about the Toyota Land Cruiser with the potentially child-killing bull bars and just how a wasps' nest managed to establish itself in the boot. And it wasn't like it was my idea in the first place – a ghost told me to do it.

We only go ten metres down the road when Simon pulls me into a gap between two houses which turns out to be an alleyway. He's very strong and I'm not sure I could break his grip – I'm seriously considering drastic measures when we emerge onto another road and he lets go of my arm.

'Would you like to come home for tea?' asks Simon.

'Where do you live?'

He points to a big semi-detached house further up the road. Belsize Park, where he told the Feds he lived, is way to the south.

'You lied to the Feds,' I say.

He shrugs but says nothing, just stands there and waits for me to answer the question.

'Yeah all right,' I say. 'Tea.'

He smiles and he's got this peng* smile which lights up his whole face and shows perfect white teeth. You can't fight a smile like that. You can only hope that its owner has sworn an oath to only use it for good.

* According to my great-niece – 'Handsome, good-looking, you know – attractive!'

19

5

Ginger Beer

Simon stops me before we reach his house.

'Wait two minutes and ring,' he says, and takes off around the side of the house where there's a side passage to the garden, blocked with a green wooden door. Simon trots to the door and, without breaking stride, jumps up, pulls himself up and over.

Since I'm waiting I check out the house, which is five storeys if you count the basement and the attic conversion. It's built out of tan brick with what Peter calls orthogonal bay windows on the bottom two floors. Looks Victorian to me but I've been wrong before.

I've gone to birthday parties in houses like this, where everything inside is either expensive or old and the mothers stand around with fake smiles 'cause they're scared you're going to steal the furniture or something.

And they always skimp on the take-home cake, too. Which is just wrong. You should always have more cake than you'll think you need. Last time I had a birthday party, half the cake was left over and we ended up feeding it to the old dears that live on the estate.

Because my mum has to stay at home with Paul all day she knows all the old dears, and their care workers,

20

by name. They liked the cake, which Dad bought in the big Sainsbury's down Camden.

I check my fake Swatch and see that it's been two minutes and I walk up the steep steps to the front door. It's got a brass knocker and posh-looking doorbell – which I push. It rings. A little bit later I can hear shuffling from behind the door, then a grunt and then it opens.

A grown-up is standing in front of me, a Filipino woman in a blue polyester dustcoat who's so short that she can only stare down her nose at me because the top step I'm standing on is lower than the level of the ground floor.

'Yes?' she says.

I ask if Simon is in.

'Simon?' she says and frowns.

'Yes,' I say. 'Simon.'

'Oh, Simon,' she says, and suddenly she smiles. 'You'd better come in.'

She turns and walks to the bottom of the stairs and shouts Simon's name.

'There is a girl here to see you!' she calls.

She has left the door open so I cautiously step inside. The interior is what I expected, wood flooring, an antique coat-and-boot stand, walls painted light brown and with pictures nailed to it at carefully spaced intervals.

The woman calls Simon again and I leave the door open behind me – just in case.

There is a rapid thumping from above – someone is running down the stairs.

'Coming!' yells Simon.

He arrives – running down the final flight and jumping the last five steps to land in front of the woman.

He turns to me and flashes the peng smile again.

'Hello, Abigail,' he says, and turns the smile on the woman. 'This is Abigail – she's come for tea.' Then to me. 'This is Angelica who does.'

The words 'Does what?' come out of my mouth before I can stop them.

'Housekeeper,' says Angelica.

There is a big kitchen at the back with expensive granite counters and cupboards that aren't made from laminated chipboard. From a huge American fridge Angelica, after asking if I have any allergies, doles out a bottle of ginger beer and a plate of sandwiches with cling film stretched across the top. From a pair of biscuit tins come one pile of custard creams and another of chocolate Bourbons. I get to carry the bottle and the glasses while Simon is entrusted with the plates. He takes them with a solemn expression and leads me up the stairs.

Simon's room is all the way at the top of the house, and is basically the whole attic conversion with stairs that come up through the floor. I freeze when I get to the top because I can't believe how much stuff he has. Beside the cupboard and the wardrobe, there are shelves of books and board games and piles of boxes and toys in the corners or leaning precariously against the walls. He has an elevated bed with a desk and computer tucked underneath, with a separate shelf for all his schoolbooks. He has so much stuff that if you moved it to my room you wouldn't be able to get in the door.

Simon carefully puts his tray on the red lid of a storage box. Through the box's translucent sides I can see it is filled to the brim with Lego. He crosses over and opens the front-facing windows. I notice that the rear-facing window is already open. I put my tray down next to his and walk over to look out.

The back garden isn't all that, rectangular lawn and flower beds looking small from this height. It's dominated by a big tree whose branches reach all the way to the attic. But beyond the garden is the green swell of Kite Hill – Simon has the whole of the Heath as his back garden.

We have a balcony at home but mostly we use that to store stuff.

I get a strange feeling like I want to bite something, but I don't know what I should bite, so I shake it off and think instead about the way Simon made me wait before ringing the bell. I look down the length of the tree and see where a rope ladder leads up into the lower branches. From there you could climb up the branches until you were level with the window and . . .

I see a scuff mark on the tiles just to the right of the open window. It's only a metre jump from the nearest branch to the roof, but there's nothing to catch you if you fall. I look back at Simon, who is sitting cross-legged beside the Lego box and pouring himself a glass of ginger beer.

'Did you climb in through the window?' I ask.

Simon nods and slurps his ginger beer.

I wait for more but he just takes another slurp.

'Why?'

'I'm not supposed to go out on my own,' he says.

'But you do anyway?'

He nods again.

I look out at the gap between the roof and the branch and the ten-metre drop to multiple injuries – if you're lucky. The only way I'd make that jump was if the house was on fire.

'Every day?'

He shrugs and slurps.

'I wanted to meet Jessica,' he says.

I sit down opposite him, open my backpack and take out my notebook.

'What's that?' he asks.

'I like to write things down.'

'Why?

'So I don't forget them,' I say, and he nods as if this makes total sense to him.

I drink some ginger beer, find my place in my notes and ask if Simon sneaked out to see Jessica today. He says he did and when I ask him when he'd last seen Jessica he says yesterday, so I ask him how.

'She rang the doorbell,' he says, and tells me that Jessica, a girl he'd met once in the playground when he was young, said she was looking for people to come to a happening on the Heath.

6

Simon's Mum

We are playing Risk on a board so old that it has wooden pieces and the box it comes in is held together with sellotape. It's the fourth board game we've played, not counting Mouse Trap, which really isn't a game but more an excuse to build that mousetrap and the only one Simon has come close to beating me at. He can read providing he sounds out the words and he can do maths on paper and fingers – but he does everything slowly. I've checked out his bookshelves where there are rows of books like *Seraphina* and *Harry Potter* and *Huckleberry Finn*, none of which, judging by the spines, have even been opened. I guessed the books he actually reads are the ones scattered around his bed and on the windowsills. Those were Roald Dahls, *How to Train Your Dragon* and every single *Diary of a Wimpy Kid* ever written – all with cracked spines, drink stains and folded-over pages. Obviously he likes to read – he just isn't very good at it.

On his desk are the same GCSE Latin textbooks that I use. Mine are second-hand but his are as clean and as untouched as the copy of *Oliver Twist* that sits next to them or the neat pad of lined A4 next to that.

He's good at Risk, though, and he knows about the

Australia gambit even if it doesn't work that well. We need a couple of other players so we can gang up on them.

So we're playing Risk when Simon's mum comes home, stomps up the stairs and gives me the eye. She's wearing an expensive black pinstripe skirt suit, the jacket undone to reveal a blue collarless blouse. There is a thin gold chain around her neck and a matching slimline watch on her left wrist. The suit is slightly rumpled and she is breathing hard and sweating from running up the stairs.

'Hello,' she says. 'Who are you?'

Simon leaps up and hugs his mum and she's hugging back while still giving me the eye because she's wondering, *Who's this strange black girl and what's she doing in my son's room?*

'This is Abigail,' says Simon, and lets go so he can jump back to stand next to me, beaming. 'She's my friend.'

'How lovely,' says Simon's mum. 'Where did you meet?'

'I went to the shop,' says Simon. 'For Angelica.'

This is either a really good lie or a really bad one, depending on whether Simon really did run an errand for the housekeeper earlier today. 'Cause one thing I can tell for certain is that Simon's mum is going to check.

'Well, thank you for coming round, Abigail,' says Simon's mum. 'But it's getting late so I think perhaps you should go home.'

'Mum,' says Simon in a whiny voice that makes him sound five and makes his mum frown.

'It's eight o'clock,' says his mum in a crisp head

teacher voice which she turns on me. 'I'm sure your parents want you back.'

As his mum herds me down the stairs, Simon asks her whether I can come play tomorrow.

'That depends on whether you do your homework or not,' she says.

When we are at the front door, Simon's mum frowns at the darkening sky and asks me whether I don't want to call my parents and have them come fetch me. I say I don't have a phone because there's no way I'm letting her see my clapped-out Samsung and weirdly that seems to cheer her up. She offers to 'run' me home in her car but I tell her I'll be fine.

'Are you sure?' she asks reluctantly.

'Sure,' I say.

7

Stuff You Need to Know

You don't actually have to cross the Heath to get from Simon's house to mine. It's probably quicker to walk down to South End Green and catch a 46 to the end of Prince of Wales Road, but I like crossing the Heath in the dark. The trick is to be faster and quieter than any potential mugger, child molester or general wasteman and there's a thrill to it.

You don't have to go over the top of Kite Hill, either. But I like the view.

So I'm running up the path that climbs the back of the hill, and I'm trying this trick I read about where you place your heel down first and roll over your foot instead of just slapping it down. Do it right and you run through the night as silent as a ghost, with just your heartbeat and the rush of the wind in your ears.

'Oi!' calls a voice behind me. 'Hold up!'

I'm more annoyed than frightened, because you'd have to be Usain Bolt to beat me up this hill – and I'm thinking he's got better things to do than chase me. I lean into the run, flinging my hands behind me the way Molly does, and fly up the hill.

'Hold up – I need to talk to you!' calls the voice behind me, much closer than it should be.

I push harder, abandoning the silent run and the jet plane arms and concentrating on pumping my legs as fast as possible. Ahead is the brow of the hill, a dark hump against the light-polluted sky.

'Abbey Girl, stop!' cries the voice and it's right on my heels, but I finally twig what's following me up the hill. I slow up a bit, but I don't stop until we're standing right at the top of the hill by the metal panorama plaque that tells you what all the landmarks are called. There are at least a dozen olds up here, walking their dogs or drinking beer and watching the view over London.

'Not here,' says the voice from down by my feet, and I feel the brush of fur against my calves as the speaker tries to hide behind my legs. 'Somewhere where there's fewer dogs.'

Too late – a white and black collie is padding towards us, tail down, head cocked to one side, eyes bright. Weird eyes, I notice, one dark, one light. Its nose wrinkles as it sniffs.

'Listen, you sheep shagger,' hisses the voice. 'Any closer and you're going to get yourself sanctioned.'

The collie stops, but I can see a shaggy Labrador zeroing in.

'Shit,' says the voice. 'A gun dog – quick, pick me up.'

The Labrador is passing the collie, head down, intent, tail swishing back and forth.

'*Quick!*' says the voice.

Sighing, I reach down and grab the fox at my feet and pull it up into my arms. It's heavy, twenty kilos at least, twice what a normal fox would weigh. It rubs the top of its head under my chin as I try to find a comfortable way to hold the squirming animal. The Labrador and the collie have stopped advancing and are looking at us with a *Them humans is crazy* look. I reckon the dogs know exactly what I'm carrying, but fortunately up in the growing darkness on Kite Hill their owners do not.

'Let's exfiltrate to a safe location,' says the fox. 'Before I wet myself.'

*

We are sitting on a bench next to the path that runs a hundred metres downslope of the main one across the summit. It's shadowed by trees and bushes, and if people see us they'll just think I'm a crazy person talking to my dog.

The fox is sitting in my lap and still nuzzling my chin, which is beginning to vex me so I tell it to stop.

'Don't you like that?' says the fox. The voice is slightly wheezy and pitched high. I suspect this is a vixen. 'In training they said it promoted co-operation in humans.'

'Not if you don't stop,' I say, and the vixen stops. I ask her name.

'Complicated,' she says, and I say, 'That's a funny name.'

'Names are complicated,' she says. 'But you can call me Indigo.'

It's full dark now but there's enough light pollution to make out the kids' playground and the athletics track at the bottom of the hill. An Overground train is running into Gospel Oak Station and an ambulance is racing in the opposite direction down Mansfield Road – heading for the Royal Free with its blue and white light bars silently flashing.

I find I'm idly scratching the soft fur on Indigo's neck, which she seems to like.

'What do you want, Indigo?' I ask.

'I'm supposed to brief you on things you need to know,' she says, and stretches her neck so I can reach her throat.

I've met these talking foxes before. They look like *Vulpes vulpes* but they're much bigger. And because they can talk, that means they must have a different voice box and throat arrangement. And they can hold a sustained conversation, which indicates human levels of intelligence. Although, to be fair, I've met some bare stupid people who could have a conversation, so that might not prove anything.

'Who wants you to brief me?' I ask.

'Control,' says Indigo.

'And who's Control when he's at home?'

'Control is she who gives me orders.'

'Is she a fox?'

'Well, I'm not about to take orders from a cat, am I?'

'What are you supposed to tell me?' I ask.

Indigo squirms a bit, rubbing her face against my shoulder.

'Do the scratchy thing again,' she says.

So I do and she tells me that there's something growing in or around the Heath.

'Growing like what?' I ask. 'Like a tree, an animal, a fungus?'

'It's a something,' says Indigo. 'No physical shape and no smell but it's "wrong" and it affects humans, young humans.'

'Okay,' I say soothingly, because I can feel Indigo getting agitated under my hand.

'It's getting stronger,' she says. 'But we can't pin it down because it's a human thing, not a fox thing.'

'Is that why you're telling me?' I ask. 'You want me to do something?'

'We want you to keep your nose in the wind for us.'

'Why me?'

'Because you're on the list of human assets in this sector.'

'That's not actually an explanation, is it?'

'It's a short list,' says Indigo, and nuzzles my neck again. 'And you've got connections with the world of magic.'

'Wait – is this something to do with the missing kids?'

'I don't know,' says Indigo. 'We're not good at invisible stuff. We like things we can smell, or bite, or eat – especially eat.'

'What do you eat?'

'Everything,' says Indigo. 'We're omnivores.'

*

I'm in my bedroom, which is about the same size as Simon's mum's downstairs guest loo. When I got back my mum was asleep on the sofa, but she woke up when she heard me come in and I helped her bath Paul. I think he likes it better when there's two of us giving him a bath 'cause we can mess about a bit. He can't talk any more but he can still smile, sort of, so you know when he's having a laugh. Once Paul was settled and my mum had gone back to sleep in front of the TV, I went to my room to make notes and think about foxes and missing girls.

The news is wall-to-wall Rushpool-this and Rushpool-that, with Rushpool in big blood-red letters over *that* picture of the two little white girls wearing matching sun hats. There's nothing on Google News about Jessica and Natali, but when I check the Metropolitan Police website there is a notification that both girls had been returned to their homes safely.

Returned to their homes safely was standard Fed speak and tells me nothing. I'm wondering whether they were found and returned home or they returned themselves home. There was definitely something sus* about the way Natali came round to see me and Jessica recruited Simon. I stick on the word 'recruited' because I realise that's what it was – me and Simon were being recruited – but for what? The foxes think something is wrong, and the foxes have been right before – one warned me that there was trouble across the river and the next thing you know a tower block in Elephant and Castle gets blown up. Yeah, Skygarden, that's what I'm talking about.

We still don't know where the talking foxes come from, what they think they're up to, or why they're up in my business. I gave one half a Greggs sausage roll once. Maybe they imprinted. I don't know.

Paul is restless. I can hear him shifting about through the wall that separates our bedrooms. I am listening in case he wakes up and Mum needs help, but he settles down.

Natali and Jessica have been returned to their families.

---

* Short for 'suspicious' but with overtones of wrongness and outrage. Young people seem to be able to pack a great deal of meaning into a single syllable.

Mr and Mrs Fed will have filed the case and gone on to something else.

Tomorrow I'll keep my nose in the wind – it's not like I've got anything better to do.

8

The Gap Between the Branches

Simon is leaning on the fence at the top of Parliament Hill and when I ask him who he's waiting for he says me. Which is surprising, since I hadn't planned to come out this morning. I had been planning to stay in bed instead, but Paul was restless and I knew if I stayed in the flat I'd soon be up and helping Mum. I told her I was going to the library but that was really Plan B if Simon wasn't home.

Library is always a good excuse, because if Mum calls I can pretend that I have my phone on silent.

I join Simon at the railing and ask whether he climbed out the window again, and he smiles shyly – which I take as a yes.

'Aren't you worried you're going to fall?' I ask.

'No,' he says. 'Did you know there's a fox in that bush?'

'Yes,' I say.

'He's watching us,' he says.

'It's a she,' I say. 'A vixen.'

'How do you know that?'

'She told me last night,' I say.

Simon's face is a pleasant blank – which I've learnt is him thinking about something. And when he thinks

35

about something he thinks about it properly, so I'm not that surprised when he says –

'So it's a talking fox.'

'Yes,' I say. 'Her name is Indigo – why don't you say hello?'

I've done my research so I know that foxes have wicked hearing and that Indigo has been following every word I've said. She's hidden pretty deep in the bush but when I look over she's giving me a definite bad look. The look gets even worse when Simon walks over and crouches down to introduce himself.

Good, I'm thinking, let's see if *you* can resist the smile.

A white goth girl I recognise from school walks past me and then stops by the big *Welcome to the Heath* sign. I don't know her name but she's in year 11[*] and has freckles, a black frock coat and knee-high boots. She is checking her phone and looking around like she's waiting for someone. She starts looking at me with a puzzled expression, and I think maybe she's wondering whether I'm who she's supposed to meet. She is raising her hand to wave hello when a boy walks up to her and introduces himself. He's white, overweight, brown-haired, wearing a blue *Save Our* Seas T-shirt and knee-length red canvas shorts. I check his shoes – generic black trainers. He's talking and Goth Girl is nodding. Then they turn and walk off, north, towards the barrows. I have an idea.

'Indigo,' I say without looking in her direction. 'Follow the girl in black and tell me where she goes.'

Simon yelps and fur brushes the backs of my calves as Indigo races along the railings and vanishes into the

---

[*] High school sophomore.

bushes on the other side. I'm proper speechless because I never expected Indigo to do what I said, and now I'm thinking of the possibilities . . . which are endless.

Simon sits back on the railing beside me.

'Do you want to climb trees?' he asks.

*

'Jump!' calls Simon. But it ain't going to happen – no way.

I'm standing on a limb six metres up a tree in Kenwood with one arm tight around the trunk because, this far up the tree, the branch is thin enough to wobble every time I shift my weight. I'm looking over at Simon, who is standing on the limb of a completely different tree. He's practically standing on the tip of his branch and it bows under his weight while he steadies himself by holding an even thinner branch above his head.

'Jump!' he calls.

And it's not even a jump between my branch and his, it's less than a third of a metre – more of a step really. If I'm willing to let go of the trunk and walk along to where the limb gets too thin to bear my weight. It should be easy. It looked easy when Simon did it a minute ago. But I can't seem to make myself let go of the trunk.

Probably shouldn't have looked down.

'It's easy,' he calls again. And, to prove his point, he steps back to my tree.

And slips.

It's that fast that he's dropped out of sight before I can even move.

I let go and lunge forward onto the branch. I meant to straddle it, but it's too narrow and I roll right off. I manage to lock both hands around the branch, the wood burning my palms as I find myself dangling over nothing.

I can hear Simon laughing below me.

My arms are being pulled out of their sockets and bark is scraping my hands as they slip slowly off the branch. I want to yell for help but the sound is caught in my throat. I can't pull myself up, so I'm looking for somewhere to put my feet. But looking down, all I can see is the ground. I kick forwards and backwards and suddenly my heel catches on something out of sight behind me. I try to tighten my grip on the branch above me but I'm going to slip any second.

I swing back, make a wild guess as to where the branch behind my legs is, and get my foot on it. My fingers slip but now I've got my foot braced and adjust my grip. I get my other foot on the branch and now my only problem is that I'm leaning forward and spread-eagled.

I hear Simon laugh again, somewhere below me, and look down to see him climbing up to join me. He has a big grin, despite the bruise that runs up the left side of his face from chin to eyebrow.

'Tree climbing is over,' I say, and he pouts.

9

The Lady Greets the Slave or Vice Versa

Given that I'd delivered Simon home with a black eye and a limp, I thought Angelica took it pretty well. Simon wanted to sneak in via his tree again but I wasn't having that. I was still reliving the moment when his head dropped out of sight. There's bold and then there's just being stupid.

'Did you fall out of a tree again?' Angelica asks, and gets the grin in return.

She doesn't want to let me in.

'He's not supposed to go out today,' she says. 'He's supposed to do his homework.'

'I can help with that,' I say.

Angelica gives me a suspicious look. But I've been watching how Simon gets round grown-ups, and give her an innocent smile. I practised it in the mirror last night. She frowns, but I tell her we can come down and work in the kitchen if she likes and that does the trick. Next thing we're on our way upstairs with a plate full of snacks, a bottle of Florida-style fizzy orange drink and a packet of frozen peas for Simon to hold against his bruised cheek.

Once we're done with the mini sausage rolls, the mini-salads and I'm not sure what they are but they taste of peanut butter, Simon wants to play Risk, but I pull out his Latin textbook instead. There's a Post-it note stuck to the cover that says *Do exercise 1.1 to 1.4 xxx*.

This is odd, because either Simon is older than he looks or he's starting Latin GCSE a year early. Nothing wrong with that. I started two years early – but I have motivation. If I pass my Latin GCSE I get to learn magic. Peter promised and Peter better not be lying.

More likely Simon's mum is trying to give Simon a head start.

These first exercises are easy, because they're easing you into the idea of inflection which we don't do in English no more, because we use word order instead. Once you've got your head round that, you can stick your slave in front of the woman and still have her salute him. *Femina servum salutat.* What makes it long[*] is memorising all the inflections, which change with tense and other things. I was hoping if I made it a game Simon would pick it up quicker, but he doesn't. One thing I noticed, though, is once he's got it stuck in his head, there it stays.

*

Angelica has obviously told Simon's mum that I'm in the house and we can hear her doing the mad step up the stairs. The staircases in these old houses creak and each thump on a riser is followed by a creak. The angry thump-creaks are getting closer and I look at Simon,

[*] This is contemporary youth slang for 'hard' or 'difficult' – presumably because their attention spans are so truncated that mastering any task of even moderate difficulty is seen as taking an inordinate duration.

and he's giving me a superior smile and I'm wondering if it might be worth me risking that jump to the tree. It's not that I'm scared of Simon's mum, right? But a girl can get tired of being misunderstood. And if I want to be shouted at, there's a ton of elders forming an orderly queue for the privilege. Starting with my mum.

The thumping stops on the landing below as she catches her breath, and Simon jumps to his feet. He takes a classic ballet stance, second position, back straight, hands held palm-up in front of his belly.

In the silence I hear his mum take a deep breath and Simon is miming taking his own breath, hands rising as they both breathe in, before flipping over and pushing down on the exhale. Simon repeats the action twice more before miming straightening an imaginary suit jacket and flicking non-existent dust off his shoulders. I can hear his mum coming up the final flight of stairs in slow deliberate steps. Simon winks at me, scoops up his Latin homework, and as soon as his mum's head emerges through the slot in the floor he runs forward and waves it at her.

'Look, Mum,' he cries. 'I can do Latin – Abigail helped me.'

I'm impressed that she doesn't cave right away. Instead she takes the A4 pad and flicks over the answers written out in Simon's terrible handwriting. She looks at Simon, looks back at the work and then back at me. Her eyes narrow and she cocks her head to one side – but she can't be vexed with Simon because the homework is done and she has to know I'm the reason it got done.

I try the innocent look again – sooner or later it's bound to work.

She gives a little snort and invites us both down for 'supper'.

*

Simon's mum cooks exactly the same way my mum does. Banging pots and pans about as if she's angry with the ingredients and is daring them to fight her. She dishes up home-made fish fingers, peas, carrots and boiled potatoes. I'm not sure whose home the fish fingers were made in, because Simon's mum got them out of a packet.

Weirdly, she doesn't seem that bothered about Simon's bruise. She fusses a bit, but apparently this is just the latest in a long run of scrapes and bruises that Simon's been accumulating since he learnt to crawl.

'We had to sell the monkey bars,' she says, and Simon pulls a face.

For pudding we have posh peach-flavoured sorbet which, I won't lie, tastes like ice cream without the cream, but since me and Simon's mum are getting on so well right now I keep my lips zipped. After supper she's hustling me out the door, but this time she insists on driving me home.

'I'm worried about your safety,' she says, and I can't tell if she just wants to be sure I clear the area or she's genuinely concerned. If she is, I'm wondering what she knows that I don't.

I was expecting a Range Rover or something like that. But instead it's a sensible Audi with, I notice, an Airwave vehicle kit hidden amongst the other electronics.

Airwave is mainly Radio Fed, but it's also used by fire and ambulance – I'm guessing Simon's mum is Fed-adjacent in some way.

'Seat belt?' she asks and, satisfied I'm strapped in, off we go.

*

'I'm surprised that your school does Latin,' says Simon's mum one minute into the drive. 'And there was no mention of it on the website, although your creative arts programme seemed strong.'

So she'd checked the Acland Burghley website – because of course she had.

'I do it after school,' I say, which is half true.

'Interesting,' says Simon's mum. 'Why do you want to learn Latin?'

Because Peter Grant, apprentice wizard, said that if I passed my Latin GCSE then he'd teach me magic. I think he thought he was joking. But if he did, more fool him.

'So I can learn to cast magic spells,' I say to test her.

'Oh,' she says. 'Like Harry Potter?'

Which I think means she either doesn't know about the Folly, Peter Grant and Inspector Nightingale, or hasn't figured out the connection. And why should she?

'Sort of,' I say.

'Whatever gets you up in the morning,' she says.

I have her drop me off on Falkland Road so she won't know where I live.

Unlike certain foxes I could name.

Indigo is waiting for me in the garden square in the

centre of my flats. She squeezes through the fence and walks beside me as I head for my block.

'Where do you think you're going?' I ask.

'I'm coming with you,' she says. 'I'm assigned to shadow you.'

'You can't,' I say. 'My mum will freak.'

'No, she won't,' says Indigo. 'Because she's not in your den – she went with your brother in a vehicle.'

I check my phone and there's a text from my mum.

Appointment brought forward see you tomorrow
dinner in the fridge.

'What about my dad?'

'At work,' says Indigo. 'Not scheduled back until second sleep.'

One of the posh white leaseholders pops out of the front door, wheeling her pushbike ahead of her. She nods politely and holds the door for me, her eyes widening as Indigo trots in beside me.

She don't say anything 'cause on the Peckwater Estate we have our leaseholders well trained.

We're in the lift, which is small and smells of spilt orange juice.

'How do you know where my dad is?' I ask.

'We have your den under continuous surveillance,' says Indigo. 'A team based out of Kentish Town Station.'

'But why?' I ask.

'Orders from Control,' she says.

'Yeah, but why does Control want me monitored?'

'That's beyond the scope of my current need to know,' says Indigo.

'You better be house-trained,' I say as I let us into the flat.

Indigo refuses to explain why I'm under surveillance, even though I give her the chicken salad my mum left in the fridge and let her sit on the sofa when we watch *The White Queen* on the TV.

She wants to sleep in my room, so I move a sofa cushion in and put it on the floor by my bed.

'Where did the goth girl go?' I ask while Indigo is making herself comfortable.

'She exited the green zone into the Brick where it sticks into the Heath and the machine men hibernate,' says Indigo, and I think she means the Vale of Health but I can't be sure.

'Who are the machine men?' I ask.

'The whirligig men,' she says, stamping down with her front paws to ensure the cushion knows its place. 'The slide men, the crash bang operatives, the barkers and change men.'

Whirligig, barker, slide – Indigo means the pitch where the Showmen rest up their rides between shows. Definitely the Vale of Health then. So if I left the Heath there – where would I be going?

Not Whitestone Pond and Jack Straw's Castle, because if you were heading there you'd stay on the Viaduct Path. Not the houses lower down, because why would you go up first.

It's too warm to get under the duvet so I lie down on top and turn the light out.

So either Goth Girl and Nerd Boy stayed in the Vale of Health, or they walked up to the top bit of Hampstead proper.

Indigo makes a breathy noise like a sigh and I close my eyes.

*

I wake up the next morning to find Indigo on the bed with me, her head resting on my hip.

'Why didn't you stay on the floor?' I ask.

'I'm not used to sleeping on my own,' she says. 'Do the scratchy thing.'

Indigo's fur is soft and she makes little whiny sounds as I scratch. It's so easy to make her happy that it's hard to stay vexed.

'What's the operation today?' asks Indigo.

'You're going back to the Heath to keep an eye on Simon for me,' I say. 'I'm going to visit the hospital and then I'm going to the library.'

10

Deeping It

I am sitting at a mahogany reading table in a library on the ground floor of a large Regency building that sits on the south side of Russell Square on the corner of Bedford Place. It's easy to walk by it, because it blends in with the terraces that line that part of the square. It has a grand entrance with SCIENTIA POTENTIA EST written above the door, a square atrium with balconies that goes all the way to the roof and is topped by the dome, and it has at least two teaching laboratories, a lecture hall, bedrooms upstairs, and a kitchen and shooting range in the basement.

It is called the Folly, and when I have passed my Latin GCSE this is where they will teach me magic.

There is a white and brown short-haired terrier sitting upright on a chair and staring at me across the width of the table. His name is Toby, and either he can smell Indigo on me or he wants a sausage. Probably both.

This place is quiet, old and forgotten. I can concentrate here – despite Toby.

I've got my notebook out and a couple of sheets of expensive writing paper because the Folly hasn't yet caught up with the discount A4 pad. The paper is smooth and dense, and I use a fountain pen because it's like writing on money. I'm making a list of all the things I know – it's a short list.

Natali comes round to recruit me – which is definitely sus in and of itself.

Jessica tries to recruit Simon – which is double sus.

Jessica and Natali both disappear long enough to become the subject of an active police inquiry – which is triple sus because the Feds don't have the manpower to roll out for teens unless there's concerns.

And then they get themselves 'returned to their families'.

But I saw Goth Girl and Nerd Boy buck up at the same meeting place Natali and Jessica told me and Simon about. Coincidence? At least I know where they left the Heath, even if Indigo said it was outside her 'operational parameters' to follow them.

The talking foxes think something sinister is lurking on the Heath and want me to check it.

Something the foxes can't track directly.

A white man walks into the library. He's dressed in an old-fashioned charcoal-grey suit, has an old-school haircut and grey eyes. He's got that effortless posh style that Simon's mum only wishes she had. His name is Thomas Nightingale, he is a detective chief inspector and is at least a hundred years old, though he don't look it. He is also Britain's only licensed, fully qualified wizard. He takes a seat next to Toby and pulls out his notebook.

'I've just had an interesting chat with a Detective Constable Jonquire,' he says.

Which is typical. I never asked him to talk to anyone – all I wanted was for him to look some stuff up on Peter's

AWARE terminal. That's the excluse* Fed internet which gives them access to the various computer systems that I'm sure some of them actually know how to use. Peter knows how to use them. Nightingale, I'm not so sure.

Obviously, I'm not authorised to use them. And, while I've memorised both Nightingale's and Peter's warrant numbers *and* their additional security passwords, I'm saving those for an emergency.

Nightingale reads my face.

'I've always found it more efficient to simply find someone who knows the answers and ask them,' he says. 'Especially when one is not sure what the precise nature of the question is.'

'Yeah,' I say. 'You're a detective inspector so people've got to answer.'

'If only that were the case,' he says.

'Anyway, did you get one? An answer?'

'There are no current missing persons cases that match the criteria you specified,' he says. 'However, there were twenty-three reports in the last three weeks, which is what triggered the operational response you witnessed. But all of them have been resolved.'

All the kids were between the ages of twelve and sixteen, had been missing no more than two nights, and a maximum of three of them had been missing on the same nights. Nightingale is thorough, so he'd asked whether there'd been follow-up interviews. But apart

---

* Much like the youth of my own generation, today's young people have taken to amputating the ends of words. Presumably so they can speak them faster and with greater emphasis. Thankfully they have yet to take up the antipodean habit of adding an 'o' to aid flow. In any case, 'excluse' is short for 'exclusive'.

from Natali, Jessica and two other recent teenagers, none had been taken.

Nightingale draws the line at showing me the interviews or giving me the names of the other two teens.

'That information is confidential,' he says. 'And this is not our case.'

I say I understand, but I don't think he believes me because he says that if I find out anything 'interesting' I should call him.

'No worries,' I say.

'Before you do anything precipitate,' he says.

11

Legwork

My Samsung may be krutters* but I can still access Facebook. I know Natali's surname and the area she lives in – the 168 has barely made it to Euston Station and I have enough information to narrow her house down to one of three on Savernake Road. I bale the bus at Camden and hop on a 24.

Savernake Road runs down the southern side of the Overground tracks from Hampstead Station to Gospel Oak. On the other side of the line is the Heath, and I wonder if that's significant. But without the other kids' addresses I can't check it.

It's fifteen minutes later and I'm standing outside a house I realise I still recognise from a birthday party I went to eight years ago. It's another Victorian semi, but a scale down from Simon's house. This is the mid-rent version although, according to Zoopla, houses on this side of the street, with back views over the Heath, go for a million more than houses on the other side.

The white stucco on the gatepost is grimy and cracked and the front garden has gone a bit wild. The porch is freshly painted, though, and it has one of those Number

* Ugly, unpleasant.

51

10 doors with an ornamental knocker that looks like it should have the face of a dead banker but doesn't.

I ring the doorbell and wait.

A white man opens the door, a shrunk version of the Natali's dad I remember from eight years ago. He's wearing a black T-shirt with THE CLASH written across the front over a red Soviet-style star, black jeans and a hostile expression. He tries to look friendly when he sees me, but he's too pissed off to make it convincing.

'Can I help you?' he says, and I ask whether Natali is in.

'Yes,' he says. 'But she's not allowed visitors.'

'I'm sorry to hear that,' I say. 'I just need to ask her a few things for a school project. I won't take long – I promise.'

Natali's dad hesitates, but the aura of the school project exerts a powerful influence on posh grown-ups. My mum would have wanted to know details – what project? Which school? But Natali's dad is too worried about seeming rude to a child to ask questions. Plus I think he sort of recognises me.

He doesn't invite me in, though – makes me wait on the doorstep while he fetches Natali.

Natali is looking pale and booky* in pink pyjama bottoms and an oversized Sex Pistols T-shirt that she must have borrowed from her dad. She's surprised to see me. 'Abigail,' she says. 'I haven't seen you for years.'

We're back in sus-land, then. But what kind of sus is it?

* Unless I'm mistaken the best translation for this instance would be 'wan', although Abigail herself insists on 'dodgy'.

'You came down my ends two days ago,' I say. 'You invited me to a happening on the Heath.'

'I don't remember,' she says.

Not *No I didn't,* which is what you would say if you were denying things.

'Really?' I ask.

'Yeah,' she says. Leaning closer as if she don't want anyone else to hear. 'They say I was . . .' She hesitates and leans in even closer and whispers, 'Missing.'

'Missing how?' I whisper back.

'I don't know.' She shakes her head. 'I don't remember anything.'

'What – nothing?'

'I remember a kitchen. Maybe . . .' Natali shrugs.

'Natali!' Her dad is calling from further along the hall.

'Dad doesn't believe me,' she says in a normal voice, on purpose I reckon, so that her dad can hear. 'He never believes me about anything.'

'I believe you,' I whisper, and I'm a bit surprised to find I mean it. 'Add me on Snapchat.'

And then I give her one of my disposable identities that I use when I want to keep people at arm's length. Which, if truth be told, is most people most of the time.

'When they give me my phone back,' she says.

Now her dad is walking back up the hall to loom at Natali's shoulder and make it clear that our conversation is over. I give him another attempt at Simon's smile and thank them both.

The door is barely closed behind me when I hear them shouting.

I walk down the path and I'm not even through the gate and my phone is ringing. I check and the screen is showing an unknown number. I answer and immediately recognise the voice – Simon's mum.

'Abigail,' she says. 'Is Simon with you?'

'How did you get my number?' I ask.

'That's not important right now,' she says.

In the background I can hear elders chatting quietly. Their voices sound flat, as if Simon's mum is inside a recording studio and there's sound baffling.

'What makes you think he's with me?'

'Is he?'

'No.'

'He was definitely in his room this morning,' says Simon's mum. 'And Angelica heard someone calling his name.'

'So,' I say, 'what about his other friends?'

'He doesn't . . .' she starts to say. Then, 'His other friends are all away on holiday. Are you sure it wasn't you?'

No, I went round, called him out to play and totally forgot I did it, which I do not say, because now I'm getting suspicious. What if Jessica or someone like her has been out to recruit Simon again?

'Did Angelica say where the voice was coming from? The front or the back?'

'What are you thinking?'

'Front or back?'

There is a pause as Simon's mum thinks about it. I like that she takes me seriously, but it's not always a good thing. If the olds are paying attention, you've got to be careful about what you say in front of them.

'From the back garden,' she says and then, while I'm still thinking it out, 'Do you know where he is?'

'Maybe,' I say, but really I know for certain. 'If I see him I'll send him home.'

'I'd much rather . . .' says Simon's mum, and pauses for a moment. 'If you happen to run into him, could you perhaps bring him home?'

'No worries,' I say.

'Good,' she says and hangs up.

I add the number to my contact list as SIMON'S MUM.

'All right then,' I say loudly. 'You two can show yourselves.'

12

Surveillance Op #01

I turn to see Simon come out from where he was hiding behind a blue Renault. He has a lead in his right hand and at the other end is Indigo – wearing a collar. They both trot over and give me identical innocent looks.

'Why are you following me?'

'We wanted to know where you were going,' says Indigo, and Simon is nodding agreement.

I point at the lead.

'Are you wearing a collar?'

'Good, isn't it?' says Indigo. 'I'm undercover as a dog. Lets me move about in the Brick in daylight.'

What she looks like is a big fox wearing a collar. If she isn't on Facebook in the next hour I'll be really surprised.

'Was this part of your training?' I ask.

'Nah,' says Indigo. 'Simon thought of it.'

Simon gives me that grin – you could use it to guide jets in at Heathrow.

'Okay, Indigo,' I say, and start walking back towards the footbridge. 'Let's get you under proper cover.'

'For operational reasons,' says Indigo, 'you should call me Gaspode.'

'Gaspode?'

'That's my cover name,' says Indigo. 'Part of my legend.'

'Def going to be legendary if you don't get off the street,' I say.

We walk quickly to the footbridge across the railway line. There's a dog waste bin here, and in the heat the slope up to the stairs stinks of shit and wee. Indigo lists the dogs whose markers she can smell. Not what their owners call them, unless there are really three dogs called George H-19, George H-15, George H-26.

'All gun dogs are designated George,' says Indigo. 'The H stands for Heath and the numbers are allocated sequentially.'

We walk across the bridge and Indigo explains that collies are Sugar Dogs, dachshunds, terriers and other dogs bred to catch rats are Rogers, while German shepherds were designated Ables, although Indigo didn't know why.

'Why aren't the gun dogs called Golf,' I ask, because that's the phonetic alphabet for G, but Indigo says that G is for George. I recite the standard alphabet to Indigo and Simon as we head up the hill towards the Parliament Hill entrance, where we all met.

'Where are we going?' asks Simon.

'I'm going to the Vale of Health,' I say. 'But you might want to go home.'

Simon pulls a sour face.

'It's going to be boring,' I say.

His face scrunches up.

'Why?' he asks.

*

'This is so boring,' says Indigo.

'Why are *you* bored?' I ask. 'Aren't you trained for surveillance?'

We're sitting on a bench opposite the Showmen's* winter quarters. From here we can watch the entrance to the Vale of Health. Indigo says this is where Goth Girl and Nerd Boy left the Heath. Because it's summer, the winter quarters are mostly empty and I can easily watch both routes off the Heath, as well as along the path that runs past the Vale of Health Pond.

'Still boring,' she says.

But it turns out Simon isn't bored. Because Simon loves to people-watch – as long as I make up stories about them. Or, if necessary, I get him distracted by letting him play *Angry Birds* on my phone. He's not allowed a phone.

'You should call Childline,' I said when he told me.

'Can't,' he said. 'Don't have a phone.'

His face was so serious it took me at least fifteen seconds to work out he was making a joke.

A fat white girl jogs past in yellow leggings, expensive white trainers and purple Lycra crop top – a phone strapped to her upper arm, the headphone cable flexing with every step. Her hair is dripping with sweat and she's breathing hard, but her expression is far away and I wonder what she's listening to and feel a bit jealous.

Simon nudges me – he wants a story.

'Alien,' I say. 'Trapped on Earth when her starship

* Showmen is the collective noun for those who live an itinerant life taking attractions from fair to fair. The equivalent term in the US is 'carny'.

58

crash-landed in the Model Boating Pond. She's not running for her health but 'cause she's got to find a missing bit of her ship that fell off during the crash.'

Indigo makes a noise halfway between a sneeze and a laugh.

'Are there aliens?' Simon asks Indigo.

'Not that I know of,' she says. 'Unless you count cats.'

'Cats are aliens?' asks Simon, but I'm not listening because I've got a shiver and a sensation like someone's waving an open tin of Whiskas under my nose.

Then somebody starts screaming.

13

Rushing In

I am running towards the screams.

I've been warned about this, by Nightingale. Just after he had a sit-down with my parents regarding my extracurricular ghost-hunting activities. Not a coincidence.

'Bravery and a desire to help are all very commendable,' he said. 'But, when rushing towards the action, one should be cognisant that there might come a point where one should stop rushing and take cover.'

'Take cover from what?' I'd asked, and made a mental note to look up 'cognisant' later.

'Ah,' said Nightingale. 'Perhaps "take cover" was not quite the right term. It's important to have some understanding of what precisely it is one is dealing with before you take action. You don't want to inadvertently put yourself or anyone else at risk.'

What I'm looking at right now is a fight between the Cat Lady, who is the one doing the screaming, and Nerd Boy, who is shouting. The Cat Lady's all-terrain shopping trolley has fallen over to scatter plastic food containers and cardboard boxes across the path.

The Cat Lady has both hands locked around Nerd Boy's upper arm while he desperately tries to pull free.

He is shouting, 'Get the fuck off me!' and pushing at the Cat Lady with his free hand.

I am less than two metres away when he balls his fist and punches the Cat Lady square in the face.

'Hey!' I shout.

Nerd Boy whips his head around to look at me.

'Help me!' he yells, and punches the Cat Lady in the face again. The Cat Lady lets go of his arm, staggers backwards and sits down hard on the path. Her hands are pressed to her nose.

I skitter to a halt in front of Nerd Boy and realise that I have no idea what to do next.

'She attacked me,' he says, and flinches as Simon arrives at my side.

'Stay there,' I say, and crouch down by the Cat Lady to see if she's all right.

'She's mental,' says Nerd Boy.

'That's not a nice thing to say,' says Simon.

I ask the Cat Lady if she's okay and quick as a flash she grabs my wrist – she's incredibly strong. Close up she smells of cat food, old clothes and something else – an electric ozone smell.

'Beware the Pied Piper,' she hisses. 'If you follow him he'll take you to the cave of happiness.'

'Told you,' says Indigo, who is hiding amongst the long grass by the path. 'Her mind has been softened by exposure to alien cats.'

'You're not helping,' I say.

'Sirens,' says Indigo, and a moment later I can hear sirens in the distance.

Nerd Boy looks around, panics and runs away.

'Do you want me to catch him?' asks Simon.

'No,' I say. 'You and Indigo run and hide – stay away from the Feds.'

Both boy and fox ask me who the Feds are at the same time.

'Police,' I say, and add that his mum isn't going to like it if they start asking her questions. That's enough to scare him off, and Indigo darts after him.

'Who's the Pied Piper?' I ask the Cat Lady, who has let go of my wrist and is prodding at her nose – which is not bleeding. She looks surprised now, rather than angry. But it doesn't seem she wants to get up. I repeat my question, louder, and she turns to look at me.

'Man with a flute,' she says. 'Lures away rats and children.'

The siren is getting louder.

'What's he look like?'

'Man in red and yellow, red and yellow with a flute and dancing feet.'

'Did you see him?'

'Don't be daft,' said the Cat Lady. 'Nobody sees him. But they hear him, yes they do. They hear him and they follow him to the cave of happiness.'

The siren stops and I look up to see a white Ford Fiesta pull up. It has a light bar on its roof, yellow and blue police livery and the word CONSTABULARY written across the bonnet.

'Do you know where the cave is?' I ask.

'On the other side,' says the Cat Lady.

Two Feds get out of the car, both white men. The Heath has its own small police force, the Hampstead Heath Constabulary – they work for the City of London

Corporation and have all the normal Fed powers of arrest.

'Could you stand up, miss?' says the lead Fed.

And they have the normal Fed attitude.

'A big boy attacked her,' I say. 'And ran away.'

*

'You were a long time,' says Simon. 'We thought they'd arrested you.'

Long enough for the world to turn away from the sun and evening to start. We are walking along the causeway between Number 1 and Number 2 Hampstead Ponds – a short cut to South Hill Park Road, where Simon lives. Indigo insists on wearing her lead again – we get some strange looks but nobody has tried to chat or taken pictures yet.

'Nah,' I say. 'Feds always make you wait around while they're calling people on the radio and stuff.'

Peter says it's a feature, not a bug. No matter how rowdy someone is, if you make them stand around or sit still for half an hour they calm down. Except for the ones that don't – they get cuffed and thrown in the back of a van.

What he doesn't say is that it's a power move – the Feds' way of making sure you know they're in charge. No matter who you are, they could make you stand still, sit down and behave.

The world is rotating us away from the sun and the light is turning golden. Indigo and Simon are laughing at a black Labrador, George H-98, futilely chasing a duck on the other side of Number 1 Pond.

I manage to persuade Indigo out of her dog disguise

63

before we leave the Heath, but when we get to Simon's house I know I'm not coming in by the way his mum blocks the front door.

'You,' she says to Simon. 'Go upstairs to your room.'

Simon slinks past her but gives me a cheeky wave from behind her back.

'Where was he?' she asks me.

I give her some flannel about finding him in Kenwood, which I don't think she believes.

'Well, he's grounded now,' she says. But then she hesitates before saying that if I want to visit tomorrow, I can. 'As long as you don't go out.'

I say I might and she closes the door.

'Badger!' says Indigo, which I can tell is totally a fox insult.

14

Because Power

Demi-monde – which is French for 'half-world' and an old euphemism, according to Miss Redmayne who teaches humanities, for any sexually active woman who failed to conform to the strict patriarchal gender norms that permeated French society in the dark days before Tinder. Meanwhile, back in the today, the *demi-monde* is the posh term used to talk about the society of the magical adjacent. This includes people who are naturally magical, what Peter and Nightingale call the *fae*, people who can do magic, like wizards and ting, and people that hang out with them because . . . reasons. At the top of the pile are the *genii locorum*, the tutelary spirits of place. Or what my dad might call river spirits.

Not that I've told my dad about them because . . . culture.

In London these are the daughters of Mama Thames and they look like your aunty, or your cousins or a social worker, but they're not because . . . power.

Hampstead Heath lies in the arms of two branches of the River Fleet. She feeds the ponds and occasionally floods the basements of buildings from Kentish Town to Blackfriars. Peter took me to stand on the Holborn Viaduct once and pointed up Farringdon Road.

'Look at the way it curves,' he said. 'Look at the way the land slopes down to meet it. They buried it two hundred years ago and it still shapes the city.'

So if anyone was going to know what was going on on Hampstead Heath, it was going to be the River Fleet. The trick is getting her to talk to you.

*

I'm standing on the opposite side of the Heath to Simon's house, by the Highgate Number 1 Pond, which is the last in a string of ponds and the one that drains directly into the Fleet. It's noon on another hot day and the paths are full of sweaty dogs and panting joggers. Although the dogs, at least, get to jump in the pond to cool down. I meant to be up here first thing, but my dad had one of his turns and decided that, since Mum was with Paul at the hospital, he was going to cook us dinner. My dad can cook exactly one thing, corned beef hash, which consists of corned beef, rice, spare vegetables and enough pepper to ensure spontaneous combustion if you're foolish enough to eat too much. He's really proud of it so I don't like to disappoint him. So I had to wait for this morning to hit the Folly library, where I checked Meric Casaubon and Charles Kingsley on how to get the attention of a *genius loci*. I also learnt a new word. Propitiation.

Propitiation is when you sacrifice something valuable to your friendly neighbourhood deity – which is a fancy word for god – in order for them to either A: do you a favour or B: stop doing something peak* like flooding

* Apparently 'bad', although Abigail assures me that the use of 'peak' gives a greater sense of alarm than the plain English.

66

your basement or spoiling milk. People have been flinging jewellery, swords and the occasional severed head into the rivers of London for thousands of years. The Romans liked to sacrifice animals and pour away wine, but I don't like wine and I don't think Indigo would regard it as much of an honour. And anyway, she can swim. Peter says you can't go wrong with alcohol, either lager or spirits, providing it's in quantity. I considered raiding my dad's stash of Special Brew or the bottle of Gordon's gin my mum keeps on the top shelf in the kitchen.

But Kingsley makes it clear – it has to be something valuable to you personally. Properly valuable, too, and I've only got two things that aren't people that count. And I need my laptop for school.

So I pull my Samsung out of my pocket.

It was a hand-me-down from an aunty when she upgraded to a smartphone and an embarrassment at school, but it's been pretty reliable and the battery life wasn't bad.

There's a film of green pond scum stretching out three metres from the shore, so I give it a good hard throw so that it lands in clear water. I'm tempted to shout something cheeky like 'Oi, Fleet – how about a word?', but that was my phone I just sacrificed and the chances that I'll get it replaced are bare slim. In the end I don't say nothing.

Quarter of an hour later and I'm wondering how long you're supposed to wait – Kingsley and the rest never said – and maybe my phone wasn't enough. I go and sit down with my back to the fence which divides off the flats. I've got a book, a tangerine, a KitKat, a bottle of

Dr Pepper and, as soon as I unwrap the KitKat, a large talking fox.

'I thought chocolate was poisonous to foxes,' I say, holding the KitKat out of reach.

'Is it?' asks Indigo, who has climbed into my lap trying to reach it.

'Yeah,' I say. 'I looked it up – you can have some tangerine.'

'It smells so good,' whines Indigo, but settles down with her head on my chest. 'Scratchy,' she pleads.

I scratch the soft fur of her neck and chest with my right hand while eating the KitKat with the left.

A swan is passing close to the shore and Indigo's head turns to track it.

'Vicious buggers,' she says.

'Billiards,' I say.

'Who's Billy Yards?' Indigo asks, perking up. 'Who does he work for?'

'Billiards,' I say. 'It's a game. A bit like snooker.'

'What's snooker?'

'Not important,' I say.

What is important is that it's played on a big expensive fabric-covered table – it's not generally known as an outdoor sport. It's also well posh and not often played by teenagers, not even posh ones like Natali. *A happening with billiards*, she'd said. And, thinking back, that should have been a clue right there.

'If they're playing billiards,' I say, 'then they got to be indoors.'

Possibly somewhere with billiard tables.

Indigo stiffens and makes a hissing sound like a snake coughing up a furball.

'What is it?'

'Something's coming,' she whispers.

I can feel it too. A weird singing in the head, like when you walk into a room full of strangers and could swear they're all staring at you and there's nothing you can do but keep your head up and dare them to make some beef about it.

Quick as a flash, Indigo snakes off my lap and burrows into the gap between the small of my back and the fence. I can feel her trembling.

'In front of you,' she hisses.

There is a dog lying in the grass three metres to my front and left. It's a black and white collie with one blue eye and one brown eye. I recognise it as the one that approached me and Indigo that first night on Kite Hill. It is lying on its belly in the way sheepdogs do when they're waiting for instructions.

I look around to see if I can spot its owners and don't see any wizened farmers in flat caps, or anybody else taking an interest for that matter.

'Sugar Dog H-1 Alpha,' says Indigo, still trembling.

'Meaning what?' I ask.

The sheepdog's gaze is fixed on me.

'Dog captain, dog officer,' says Indigo. 'Alpha male – top dog.'

'Meaning what!'

'Meaning you wished to meet the local goddess,' says Indigo. 'Wish granted.'

15

An Island in the Aegean

As soon as there were ponds on the Heath then people started swimming in them. This being the old days, they didn't worry about Health and Safety, and if four people were dying a month during the summer that was a price worth paying. What did disturb the Victorians was that people were doing it without their clothes on.

Obviously something had to be done, otherwise people might get overexcited at the sight of some random bather's package. So, by the end of the nineteenth century, the London County Council added some proper facilities to the Mixed Bathing Pond on the Hampstead side. This became the famous 'Cockney child's seaside', where thousands of poor kids came to splash about in the summer, meaning that the posh olds needed somewhere else to swim. In 1893 the Highgate Men's Pond on the other side of the Heath was opened, and there fine strapping Edwardian men could show off their legs to their fellow men without having any females around to harsh their squee. It wasn't until 1926 that the Highgate Ladies' Pond opened further up the hill.

On the first day there was a host of donnies standing on the slope overlooking the pond, eager to catch a glimpse of the other half of the population getting wet in their scandalously skimpy swimming costumes. Never mind that they was as revealing as a burkini – it's the thought that counts, isn't that right, fam? This is probably why the pond is now screened on all sides by trees so tall you'd need a drone to see over.

And why there is a sign that says WOMEN ONLY on the front gate.

As soon as I'd got to my feet the collie had sprung up, turned smartly and headed north. I followed but Indigo stayed behind, making little whimpering noises. The collie led me past the men's pond, the Model Boating Pond and then left up the hill to Millfield Lane, which runs along the east side of the Heath. Ponds and trees on one side, the back fences of the uber-boujee* on the other. I find out later that this is also called Poet's Lane, because Keats and Coleridge used to jam down here looking for nightingales. If I'd kept going I'd have ended up in Kenwood, where me and Simon practised falling out of trees. Halfway along there is a gate in the iron fence that marks the entrance to the women's pond.

Beyond the gate is a cool shady path through the trees.

The Border collie pauses to let me catch up, watching me over his shoulder with cool mismatched eyes.

I'm not prang†, not even a little bit. What's there to be scared of, anyway? I follow the Border collie down the path, past the changing rooms and out into the sunlight again. I'm standing at the edge of the meadow that runs from the trees down to the pond. Dozens of white

* This is another import from American English and means rich and/or pretentious. Derived, it seems, from the word bourgeoise.
† According to my great-niece this means scared or possibly shaken up.

women are stretched out on their towels and sizzling like bacon in the hot sun. Most are pale but a couple are tanned. One old lady near me is nut-brown and wrinkly in nothing but a polka-dot bikini and a sun hat. She has an open hardback book lying across her face as a sun shield – I can't see the title.

The collie nudges my leg and pads forward, threading between the scattered bodies. I follow her and, as we walk deeper into the meadow, I feel the quality of the air shift around me. As we approach the far end, the colour of the sunlight deepens and thistledown swirls in a breeze off the pond that smells of the sea – which is pretty effing unlikely, given the nearest proper seaside is fifty kilometres away.

At the end of the meadow a picnic has been laid on a red and white checked cloth and a group of women lounge around, drinking white wine coolers. At their centre is a broad-shouldered and dark-skinned black woman. She is wearing an expensive blue tankini with a halter top that shows off her broad shoulders and muscled arms and legs. Her hair is shaved down to a shadow, her eyes are black, her nose is flatter than my dad's and when she sees me her mouth stretches into a Cheshire cat grin.

'Abigail,' she says, and beneath her voice is the roar of the printing press and the crackle of telegraph wires. This is the spirit of the River Fleet that rises in the heights of Hampstead and Highgate, then feeds the ponds before rushing underground beneath the Farringdon Road and joining her mother at Blackfriars. The great mechanical presses that once thundered out the news and gossip may have gone from her valley, but the spirit remains.

'What brings you to my court?' she asks, and her words draw me closer with promises of secrets and gossip, of witty conversation and smoky after-hours clubs. This is the *seducere*, also called the glamour, and these supernatural types like to try it when they meet you. It's a test. But that's okay, 'cause I've always smashed it at tests.

I've got my hands on my hips and my face set in a way that is pure my mum when someone from the council, or the school or the hospital, is griefing her.

'I've got some questions,' I say.

A woman in a pink bikini next to Fleet opens her mouth and laughs. She is long and thin and so pale she's almost blue. She has a pointy chin, a snub nose and violet eyes. Her hair is swept back and up and is as white and fluffy as the thistledown blowing off the pond.

'This is the cousin, right?' she says, uncoiling from the ground, head tilted to the side as she sways in my direction. 'Ghost hunter, fox whisperer, troublemaker.'

'Yeah,' I say, trying not to shake. 'Who are you?'

'I'm Thistle,' she says with her face right in mine. 'Dancer, shaker, swimmer – Riverwife.'

She closes her eyes and takes a deep breath through her nose like I'm something tasty. She opens her eyes and circles around me, but I'm not moving. I know better, I've read books – Thistle is *fae* and the *fae* are like cats. They like to play games.

'Not yet taken up the power,' she breathes in my ear. 'Why not?'

'I can wait,' I say.

'Liar,' she whispers in my other ear. 'But wise to wait.'

'Leave the poor girl alone,' says Fleet, and pats the ground by her side. 'Sit.'

The roar and oil stink of the printing press is all around me, and around its edges like a cloud are the ballad sheets, pamphlets, flyers, earworms, slogans, memes, likes, dislikes, follows and friends. This is the *seducere* again and it pulls at me like the sound of my mother's voice.

But I can ignore my mum when I have to, and so I stay where I am and count to ten – slowly.

Thistle laughs with a sound of little bells and Fleet narrows her eyes at me.

'All right, girl. You're a badass,' she says as Thistle slides down to wrap herself around her back, one arm draped comfortably over her shoulder. 'But I'm not standing up, so it's sit down or go home.'

16

A Localised Heat Differential

I am sitting right in the middle of the Summer Court of the Goddess of the River Fleet. Or I am sitting down to a picnic with a bunch of women in the sunbathing meadow of the Kenwood Ladies' Bathing Pond.

Maybe I'm doing both – sometimes it's hard to tell.

'Bubbly?' asks Fleet, holding out a fluted wineglass full of champagne. I know it's champagne because I can smell the alcohol. Thistle is leaning against Fleet's back, her chin resting on Fleet's shoulder – watching me, her eyes bright.

'No, thank you,' I say in my mum's posh voice – the one she uses on the telephone to the hospital.

'There's no obligation,' says Fleet. 'You may eat and drink at my table without fear.'

'No, thank you,' I say.

'Something else?' says Thistle. 'A cordial? Dewdrop, cowslip – elderflower?'

'No, thank you,' I say. Because not only don't I take chances – but, dewdrop? Seriously?

Now that I've got used to Fleet and Thistle, I start to notice the rest of the crew. They're whiter than I expected and most of them are what my dad calls *eiwashi*, which is a Themne word that means size zero skinny. A lot of them I reckon are part *fae*, but Peter says we've got to be careful about making assumptions because people come in all shapes and sizes, anyway. And thinking you know what somebody is is worse than not knowing anything at all.

'So, what do you want, Troublemaker?' says Thistle.

'To make trouble, perhaps?' says Fleet.

'I want to know what's going on,' I say.

'In general, or could you localise it a tiny bit?' says Fleet.

'The missing kids,' I say, and Fleet frowns.

'As I understand it, there aren't any,' she says. 'Has that changed?'

'Something is recruiting teenagers,' I say. 'Something weird.'

'What does the Nightingale say?' she asks. And when I don't say nothing she draws the right conclusion. 'Don't you think you should tell him?' she asks.

'When I have something to tell him, I will,' I say and Fleet nods.

'As you like,' she says. 'The world is full of invisible currents. Do you know what makes the wind blow?'

'The air flows from high pressure areas to low pressure areas,' I say, because some of us were paying attention in geography.

'Do you know what causes areas of high and low pressure?' she asks, and I'm about to say of course I do when I remember that Peter says you can learn more when you listen than when you speak. True, he's thinking of police interviewing technique, but it works for other stuff as well.

I shake my head.

'It's caused by the interaction of the radiant heat of the sun and the surface environment of the Earth,' she says, and I think she could have just said that the sun heats some places faster than others, but say nothing because . . . listening.

'And this interaction exists at multiple interrelated scales,' she says, and throws her arm in the air and sweeps her hand in a big circle. 'From the Hadley cells that drive the trade winds to the localised heat differential that creates the pleasant breeze we're enjoying now.'

And there is a cool breeze coming off the swimming pond, still with that suspiciously fresh salt sea tang.

'Isn't that you?' I ask. 'Aren't you making that happen?'

'Yes,' she says, and Thistle giggles behind her hand. 'But it's the same thing. And the wind is just one current in the biosphere. There's the currents of the sea, of the animals, of people and' – she waves her hand again – 'other things.'

'Other things?'

'Other *invisible* things.'

I'm getting bare vexed with the whole Dumbledore teaching approach here. Obviously Fleet means that the not-quite-missing kids are caught up in an invisible current but can't bring herself to just say that, because . . . who knows? Coolness, probably.

'My love,' says Fleet, reaching up to place a hand on Thistle's cheek. 'She can see the wind while I cannot.'

'Really?' I say. 'What colour is it?'

'It is the same colour as the breath you used to speak your question,' she says.

Fleet speaks quickly – trying to keep the chat where she wants it.

'I can see the flow of water through the landscape,' she says.

'You can see that?'

'Maybe *feel* would be more accurate,' says Fleet. 'Sense certainly. My point being, some currents are visible to some people and not to others.'

'But we can measure the wind,' I say. 'We don't have to see it to do that. We use instruments, don't we?'

'Precisely,' says Fleet, looking smug 'cause she thinks she's outsmarted me and made me think for myself. Olds are like this, but I know who Socrates was – he was in an episode of *Horrible Histories*.* 'But before we had barometers and anemometers and radar,' says Fleet, 'people had other ways to read the wind. Do you understand what I'm saying?'

I'm bare tempted to say no just to vex her, but I know what I need to do now and I have to be getting on with it.

'Yep,' I say and jump up. 'Thanks for all your help – laters.'

But, before I can escape completely, Thistle is at my side. She takes my elbow and draws me away from the picnic and into the cool shade of a tree.

'A word in your shell-like before you go,' she says. 'I don't want you to get the wrong idea about making a sacrifice.'

She puts her arm around my shoulder and I feel a weird thrill, but I can't tell if it's her or me. That's the trouble with the *fae* – they got bare fluid boundaries.

---

* A rather splendid BBC children's programme about history with sketches and songs. You really should 'check it' as Abigail might say.

'Whatever you sacrifice, however important it is to you personally, it doesn't put an obligation on the likes of my love,' she says, and presses something into my hand. I look – it's my Samsung. 'It just gets their attention. And that's not always a good thing.'

When I press the button on the Samsung it boots up.

'I added my number,' she says. 'But only for emergencies.'

'Thank you,' I say.

'You just remember who it was who handed it back,' she says, and lets go of my shoulders. Then she kisses me on the forehead and my mind is full of fluff and multicoloured party balloons. 'Have fun,' she says and releases me. 'Make trouble.'

17

George Oboe Sugar Charlie Fox

'm walking away from the women's pond and thinking about invisible currents.

Natali came looking for me just as Jessica came looking for Simon. Once could be an isolated event, twice could be a coincidence, but if Goth Girl had recruited Nerd Boy then we were looking at a pattern.

So, what can we tell from that?

One: Natali knew me, Jessica knew Simon – if Goth Girl knew Nerd Boy, then maybe the recruiters recruited people they knew.

Two: so far nobody had gone missing permanently, that we knew of, so people weren't being lured somewhere to have their brains sucked out. Or at least not on their first visit, anyway.

Three: first visit to *where*?

Four: none of the recruiters or their targets were olds – or even old enough to drink.* Invisible currents, said Fleet, each driven by the interaction of different forces

---

* Here in the UK one can legally drink beer or cider at home with meals from the age of 16 onwards and can purchase alcohol at 18 years old. One fears that Abigail is referring to the lower threshold rather than the higher.

and before we had proper instruments ... *People had other ways to read the wind.*

By watching the clouds, I reckon, and seeing what blew in which direction.

As I get to the top of Millfield Lane, Indigo leaps out of the bushes that surround the public toilets and into my arms.

'You're alive,' she says as I stagger. 'The dogs didn't eat you.'

Foxes, I learn, don't go into the women's bathing pond. At least, foxes don't go in twice.

'I need some surveillance done,' I say as Indigo squirms herself into a comfortable position over my shoulders.

'Came top in my class,' says Indigo smugly. 'I'm practically invisible.'

'I noticed,' I say, because she's bare heavy and if she thinks she's staying there for more than a minute she can think again. 'But I need you to cover a wide area.'

'How wide?'

'All the way around the edge of the Heath,' I say.

'The whole perimeter?'

'Is that a problem?'

'You're going to need a lot of assets for that,' says Indigo. 'I'll need authorisation from my section chief.'

'How long will that take?'

'I don't know. I've never had to get authorisation for an op that big.'

We're walking down to the east side of the Model Boating Pond because I reckon there'll be fewer people to notice that I'm carrying a talking fox around my neck.

'Normally,' she says, 'I just get assigned missions.'

'Am I a mission?'

'Affirmative.'

'Why?'

'Need to know,' says Indigo.

And obviously I didn't need to know.

I reach up and prise her off my shoulders and drop her – she lands on her feet like a cat.

'Go get authorisation,' I say.

*

I'm sitting outside the café that sits at the bottom of Kite Hill and trying to make the tea I bought with the last of my pocket money last until Indigo gets back. In front of me is Parliament Hill School, which is an all-girls ex-grammar school where parents try to send their girls so they won't have to mix with roughnecks like me at Acland Burghley. A couple of my ex-friends from primary school go there.

It's closed for the summer holidays.

The path that runs past the café goes east to west, linking the park entrances on both sides of the Heath. To my right there's the path that leads down to Gospel Oak Station, and on either side of the café are paths that run up the side of Kite Hill. It's a good place to watch for any recruited kids and to spot Indigo when she comes back from her meeting.

'Abigail Kamara?' says a voice from under my table, and I almost spill what's left of my tea.

I drop my spoon, which gives me an excuse to bend over and look. And there, sitting primly, is a vixen that is definitely not Indigo. This one is darker red, almost black around her eyes, tail and face. There are flecks of grey along her muzzle and the tips of her ears. Her eyes are a dark emerald green.

'That's me,' I say.

'If you'd care to follow me,' she says. 'Control will see you now.'

'What's your name?' I ask.

'Lucifer,' she says.

*

Foxes have slit pupils for good night vision, and so their earth* under the platform of Gospel Oak Station is dimly lit but surprisingly fresh, given that I'm surrounded by a dozen foxes – at least.

The ceiling is so low that I have to sit cross-legged with my back to the wall. One of the foxes, who Indigo calls Sugar Niner, has curled up in my lap and gone to sleep. This is vexing Lucifer because it's undermining the whole badass fox vibe, but I can tell that Indigo is trying not to laugh. I scratch the fur on Sugar Niner's back, which winds up Lucifer even more.

Golden sunlight is fighting its way through little squares of thick and dusty glass that line one of the walls just below the ceiling. Through them I can see the railway tracks curving off towards South End Green. I'm guessing that we're under the GOBLIN Line† platform but there were some proper zigzags on the way in so

---

* These are known in America as 'dens'.
† The colloquial name for the Gospel Oak to Barking Line. I must say that Miss Kamara seems very knowledgeable about the make of trains that run through Gospel Oak. It takes me back to my youth when my friends and I would gather on the Tollerton Bridge to watch the Flying Scotsman whizz by.

I can't be sure. The tunnels were fox-sized so I had to crawl past what looked like individual sleeping dens, a food store that smelt of spoiling meat and another store that was full of Tupperware boxes – contents unknown. The floor is bare, there are no cushions or straw, and when I ask Indigo why this is Lucifer interrupts to inform me that since this is the ops room, furniture would be inappropriate.

'Also, people used to fight over the cushions,' whispers Indigo.

The other foxes are gathered into groups of two or three, heads close together, whispering. Occasionally one will turn to give me a sly look.

'You're the first chap we've ever had in here,' says Indigo. The way she pronounces chap makes me think of posh people and period dramas.

Outside the rails begin to sing and a train squeals and rattles into the station. All I can see are the wheels, but I recognise the layout as belonging to the Class 172/0 diesels that do the Barking run.

I turn back to find a new fox sitting in the centre of the room. There is nothing unusual about this fox. It's a standard rusty brown with white flashes. But it's looking at me with clever hazel eyes. All the other foxes have shut up and are sitting at attention like a semicircle of statues. Even Sugar Niner has stopped squirming and sat up. But not, I notice, bothered to leave my lap.

I think Indigo winks at me but it's hard to tell.

'I take it you're Control, then?' I ask to break the silence.

The fox cocks its head to one side and narrows its eyes.

'I need to track the kids,' I say.

The fox continues to give me a cool look.

'Either you're going to help me or you're not,' I say. 'It's down to you, innit?'

Real talk – we stared at each other for the most minutes until suddenly the New Fox says, 'Mission authorised,' and turns and vanishes into the gloom.

The other foxes all relax and Sugar Niner yawns and snuggles down like it's going to go back to sleep.

'Don't get comfortable,' I say. 'You've got work to do.'

18

Isochrone

Mum and Dad are asleep on the sofa in the living room with the TV on. Even from Paul's room I can hear Ian Beale pleading with Denise to give him one more chance. I wouldn't. But then I wouldn't have stuck myself with someone that pathetic in first place.

Paul makes a noise – it's all he's got left, but I've taught myself to understand him and he wants me to keep reading. I tune out *EastEnders* and concentrate on *Reaper Man* by Terry Pratchett. It's his favourite and I could do most of it off by heart, except it makes me cry at the end because now I know what magic can really do and what it can't.

I *was* going to spend this evening making an iso-chrone map of the area around the Heath. It's from the Greek *isos* meaning equal and *khronos* meaning time, and basically you work out the area you can reach travelling by a certain mode for a certain length of time from a single point. In this case, fifteen minutes by foot from the edge of the Heath. Fifteen minutes, because I reckon that any longer than that and the Feds would have spotted one of their mispers* on CCTV, and Mr and Mrs Fed wouldn't have had to randomly harass law-abiding young ladies like myself. But Mum wanted to watch the six o'clock news and she looked so peaceful with her head on Dad's shoulder, like they were teenagers, that I reckoned Paul could wait a bit for his bath.

Paul makes a sudden *ugh* sound and bangs his shoulder on the padded bars that stop him rolling off the bed.

'Do you want me to read this or not?' I ask, and he quietens down.

I discovered isochrones on the internet when I was still in primary school and spent hours mapping out my own independent isochrone – how far I could escape from my house on foot in one hour, two hours, a morning . . .

Then I discovered the TfL site and realised I could go anywhere in the whole of London for free as long as I took a bus.† I spent a whole week and a half going everywhere – I'd pick a bus that went out into the zones and ride it all the way to the end and then all the way back. Finally, my school informed my parents that I'd been bunking off and I was grounded into the ground. I pointed out that I'd gone missing over the weekend as well, and they hadn't noticed. But that just meant my

---

* In some ways I fear the police are as bad as contemporary youth when it comes to playing fast and loose with the English language. In this particular case, 'mispers' is a portmanteau word derived from 'missing persons'.

† TfL – Transport for London is the body that runs or regulates public transport within the Greater London Area. Children under the age of eleven may travel for free, which has livened up many a bus ride, I can tell you.

mum starting crying as well as shouting. I was so happy in year 7 when the school put me in special measures because then I was going to be special too. You're stupid when you're a kid, aren't you?

I've still got my independent isochrone map hanging on my bedroom wall in an old frame I found in a skip.

Paul's independent isochrone map has been shrinking since he was five years old. All the way down to a single point centred on his bed.

So I kept reading to my brother all the way through *Holby City*, until my mum woke up to help get him ready for sleep. Afterwards she hugged me and said she loved me, and then spoilt it by saying she didn't know what she'd do without me.

Which just goes to show that elders can be just as stupid as you are.

*

It is the middle of the night and I am awake because I had a dream but can't remember what it was about. I lie in my bed and imagine I have slit pupils like a fox and can see in the dark.

Close by I can hear a big diesel locomotive revving up. Probably a Class 67 dieselelectric powering up after being held at signal outside Kentish Town Station. The Class 67 is nicknamed the Cyclops because of its single-pane windscreen. Two years ago I could have told you what the train was carrying and I would have imagined myself carried away to Tonbridge or Derby or Angerstein.

Now I know about magic.

Now I imagine seeing in the dark and running with foxes.

And maybe, somewhere out there, something that can save my brother.

It's magic, after all – anything could be possible.

19

Camp Simon's House

'It can't be easy at home, helping look after your brother,' says Simon's mum.

Which means she and the foxes have one thing in common – they're both up in people's business when they shouldn't be. I know this because I never mentioned my brother to her or Simon. I don't, as a rule, tell people unless I have to. I don't like the way they look at me afterwards – like I'm a background character in somebody else's soap opera.

To be fair, I looked her up on the internet myself. But all I found was pictures of her on other people's Facebook pages – most of them antique, and the only recent mention was of her as a senior manager at the Home Office.* I ignore her and pretend I am distracted by Simon trying to carry his camping gear out the kitchen's back door. He's got such a pile in his arms that he has to do a shimmy to finesse the doorway, and there's something about his shoulders that's making me feel bare queasy. But that ain't going to run with me, because we done

---

* As far as we can tell, Simon's mother, ███████████████ ███████████, is a Grade 7 civil servant working for the Home Office. Peter knows more and says he will explain next time you and he are facing each other in a SCIF.

puberty in year 6 and I'm starting late and I've had a chance to see how it messes with your head and makes you wavy when you should be thinking straight.

He is a boom ting, though.

*

It is a hot day and I am jamming in Simon's tent at the far end of the garden. Ahead of me is a wooden door that leads out onto Hampstead Heath, set into a two-metre wall topped with a double strand of barbed wire. This is, Simon says, to stop burglars and is the reason why he has to escape over the side door at the front. It doesn't seem to stop the foxes, who ooze through it at will.

Simon's garden is divided into two bits. The two-thirds closest to the house has a patio, a lawn and neat flower beds. There's a white enamel garden table and red wooden folding chairs. Angelica the housekeeper has promised sandwiches and ginger beer for laters.

The other third of the garden, starting about where Simon's escape tree stands, is deliberately messy with a trio of smaller trees, long grass and what Simon says his mum calls a rockery. This is obviously his bit and is littered with loads of old toys. Not far from the tent is a big plastic tank manned by a small teddy bear wearing an old-fashioned army helmet, keeping watch from the commander's hatch.

'Commander Ted,' Simon says when he spots me looking. 'Guarding the back door.'

Lucifer has taken up position behind me in the tent and Simon, now that his mum has left for work, has rushed in to get the Chubb key for the garden gate from the hiding place she thinks he doesn't know about.

'So you could have gone out of the back whenever you liked,' I said when he told me about it.

'Yes,' he said. 'But then Mum might notice and hide it somewhere else.'

Lucifer nodded in approval and said that it showed good tradecraft – no wonder Simon gets on with the foxes so well. I have my isochrone map hidden in one of Simon's sketchbooks. He has a ton of these in his room and another ton of crayons, pencils, watercolour sets although, real talk, he doesn't seem to use them much.

Still with Lucifer's help, I make a list of our assets, twenty-four foxes in all, operating in pairs for safety.

'Strictly speaking,' says Lucifer, 'a proper surveillance team should have three foxes for daylight operations – five would be better.'

But we need twenty-four teams to cover the main access points on and off the Heath – especially since we have to have what Lucifer calls 'operational redundancy' in case there is more than one set of Sugars, which is what Lucifer called the teens we were watching for.

'Sugars?' I asked.

'Subjects,' said Lucifer. 'Sugar for S, as opposed to targets which would be Tare for T.'

I actually had to deep that a bit before I realised that Lucifer was using a phonetic alphabet again, but not the one everyone uses now. When I asked Lucifer why they used that particular alphabet, she gave me a very human-looking shrug and said that it was the one the foxes had always used. Which at least was more than I'd got out of Indigo.

This was supposed to be Camp Simon's House, the

nerve centre of the combined human/fox intelligence-gathering effort – serious business, right? Up until the point where Sugar Niner and Indigo discovered Simon's garden trampoline. After a couple of experimental bounces they start doing the strange jump-dive thing foxes like to do, and then it's all of five minutes before Simon is joining in.

'I swear,' says Lucifer, glaring at the two other foxes, 'it's like herding humans. You two – we're working here.'

'I thought you guys were professionals,' I say.

Sugar Niner starts using Simon as a platform to jump from and is making delighted squeaks as he bounces.

'I blame you for this,' says Lucifer.

It's not like we've anything to be professional about for the next couple of hours, and eventually the foxes curl up in a heap at the back of the tent for a nap and only wake up when Angelica brings out tea.

'What are those?' asks Sugar Niner after Angelica has gone.

'Cheese puffs,' says Simon with his mouth full.

Sugar Niner says something but since his mouth is full of cheese puff, all I get is showered with crumbs. Lucifer rolls her eyes, but I notice she and Indigo are too busy nomming their own cheese puffs to speak.

Fortunately for me and Simon, the cheese puffs keep the foxes busy long enough for us to bags the sausage rolls and cheese and tomato sandwiches. I make Simon swap places with me and sit in the tent – I'm worried about him getting sunburnt, and I need the vitamin D.

'If you could do anything,' asks Simon, 'what would you do?'

Simon likes to ask these questions at random intervals.

The last one was if you could be any superhero, and I said Dr Manhattan and then had to explain what that was all about.

'I'd learn to fly,' I say – lying. 'What would you do?'

'Climb Nanga Parbat,' says Simon.

'Which is what?'

'A mountain in Pakistan,' he says, and explains that it's the ninth highest in the world and considered the third most dangerous to climb. But apparently this was not the reason Simon wanted to climb it.

'It's so beautiful,' he says, and I think that his mum would do her nut if she found out his plans. Or maybe she has, and that's why she doesn't like to let him out of her sight.

I'm about to ask why he thought it was beautiful but a little vixen called Zebra slinks over the garden wall and through the long grass towards us.

'Got a report,' she says once she's reached the safety of the tent.

'You've tracked one of the Sugars?' I ask.

'Not exactly,' says Zebra.

20

It Could Be a Folly

Officially it's known as the Tumulus, but everyone I know calls it Boadicea's Mount because they think she watched her last battle with the Romans from there. The archaeologists say they're wrong because (a) the last battle was further north and (b) you got to pronounce her name with a hard 'c'.

It's a big lump forty metres across that sits upslope of the Model Boating Pond and is covered in trees and bushes. Because it's a scheduled monument it's surrounded by a crusty wrought-iron fence that needs some serious love and attention. Peter and me did a *vestigia* pass on the place in the spring, but Peter wouldn't let me hop the railing to check inside. He said he'd done a historical check and the two main theories was that either it was a genuine Bronze Age burial mound or an eighteenth-century landscaping folly. It hasn't been excavated to find out, on account of it being scheduled and all that.

Foxes don't care about scheduling and neither, apparently, did wandering teenagers. Indigo leads me around to where there is a gap in the fence.

'That's where Zebra reported they go in and come out,' she says.

'Is someone tailing the last one out?' I ask.

'Of course,' says Indigo.

I follow Indigo through the gap, but Simon uses one of the benches that back onto the fence to jump over. I hear him crash through some bushes and start laughing.

'What's so funny?' I ask.

'Cut myself,' he says and, emerging from the bush, shows me the scratch on the palm of his hand. I give him some clean tissues to ball his fist around and stop the bleeding and we follow Indigo further into the bushes. I'm half expecting to run across the Cat Lady again, but instead we push out into a clearing right at the top of the mound. It's hushed and quiet and you could be in a forest for all that you can hear the outside world.

In the centre of the clearing is a silver and black microwave. A big one, the sort they use in cafés and canteens. The plug and electric cable are neatly coiled on a side bracket. The door is closed.

Simon goes to open it but I tell him no.

'Fingerprints,' I say.

Sitting in a box under my bed are the nitrile gloves that I bought to practise with my forensic kit. Peter says that the Feds always walk around with a couple of pairs in their pockets just in case. I put that on the list of things that I will start doing as soon as I get home.

I tell Simon to take off his T-shirt.

'Why?' he asks.

'I need something to cover my hands,' I say, and he gives me one of his slow looks. 'I can't take mine off, can I?' I say after a while.

For a moment I think he's going to ask me why not, but then he nods and pulls his T-shirt over his head. It's red with a white stripe across the chest and when he hands it to me, it feels expensive.

We crouch down by the microwave and I slip my hand into the T-shirt and reach out for the door.

'What do you expect to find?' Simon asks.

'Don't know,' I say.

'Maybe it's hands.'

'What?' I freeze before I touch the handle.

'Maybe it's full of hands,' he says. 'That he's cut off as trophies.'

'Get on with it,' says Indigo. 'The suspense is killing me.'

I snatch the door open – before I chicken out.

'Oh,' says Simon, and sounds bare disappointed.

The microwave is full of phones, neatly stacked to make maximum use of the space inside. Most of them are smartphones, screens dark, turned off or out of battery. A couple have LCD half-screens, also blank. I don't touch anything but it looks like the inside of the microwave is dry and the phones aren't damaged – one has a cracked screen, but that could just be wear and tear.

A scenario is forming in my mind. The kids come here, drop off their phones, go wherever they're going, then come back, pick up their phones and go home. The Feds will have been trying to track the kids' phones, but getting stuck in the big open cell area that is Hampstead Heath.

And maybe a microwave would shield them from triangulation.

I bet Simon's mum would know.

'Everybody stand up, but don't move,' I say, which

predictably causes Simon and Sugar Niner to make the same joke at the same time.

'How can we stand up if we can't move?' they both say, but I ignore them.

I tell them to stay where they are and look around to see if they can spot anything.

'Anything what?' asks Sugar Niner.

'Anything left behind,' I say.

I've been in clearings like this before, down by railway lines, behind bushes in parks, in those ignored spaces between the blocks of an estate. Normally, once the locals have found them, they get filled up with rubbish, crisp packets, used condoms, whippets, fag ends, old syringes . . . all that kind of shit. I once found a hardened steel combat knife with a twelve-centimetre blade that I passed on to Peter in case someone had got themselves jooksed by it and it was needed in evidence.

There was none of that in this clearing, which made me think that nobody was coming here to shag, do nitrous oxide or eat crisps. Just to stash their phones before they went wherever it was they were going.

Which was definitely not normal behaviour.

Simon spots it first – a splash of yellow half hidden in a bush by the desire path in and out of the clearing. I hand him back his shirt and go to have a closer look. It's a yellow cotton shirt with white polka dots, sized for a small girl. I lift it up carefully by the collar and see that the trailing edges at the front are wrinkled and twisted. Somebody had been wearing this tied up, poor white trash style. I wonder why they abandoned it. I gingerly sniff it, and smell floral body spray and a hint of sweat. Otherwise it's clean – I don't think it's been here long.

'Can one of you track this by smell?' I ask the foxes.

There is an embarrassed silence.

'The thing is,' says Indigo, 'we're not very good on smell – good at hearing . . .'

'We can orientate ourselves in relation to the Earth's magnetic field,' says Sugar Niner.

'But not really with smell,' says Indigo.

'Sorry,' says Sugar Niner.

'We need a hound dog,' says Simon, and Indigo huffs.

Holding the shirt at arm's length to minimise contamination, I pull out my phone and flip through until I find the most recently added number.

Thistle picks up on the second ring.

'Hello, Abi,' she says. 'You must want something.'

I explain what I need and she tells me no problem.

'I'll send Ziggy,' she says.

Ziggy turns out to be the collie with the mismatched eyes that the foxes all call Alpha Dog. As he trots into the small clearing I can hear the foxes scrambling to clear the area. Only Indigo is staying, and she is cowering behind my legs and making occasional squeaking noises.

Ziggy is in front of me and gives me the hard stare, so I crouch down so he can get a good look at how unimpressed I am.

'This is important,' I say. 'I need to see where this came from. Can you do that?'

According to this thing I saw on the internet, cats and dogs use expressions on us that they don't use on each other. This being on account of the fact that we effectively co-evolved together. So unless sheep are susceptible to a look of long-suffering patience, I'm going to say that the one Ziggy gave me was reserved for humans.

I hold out the yellow shirt for him, and Ziggy sniffs it a couple of times and then saunters off towards the gap in the fence. Indigo runs up my back and tries to perch on my shoulders again.

'The game's afoot!' she cries. 'Follow that dog.'

21

The House

I'm standing outside a house on a lane off East Heath Road, a four-storey semi-detached place a bit like Simon's house, only older. The house next door has a shallow roof and a half basement but this one, the house Ziggy has brought us to, is surrounded by a two-metre green wooden site hoarding and shrouded in scaffolding and plastic sheeting. There's a builder's placard halfway up, next to a blue and white sign with a drawing of a bodybuilder and WARNING ALARMED in red letters. There is an ordinary-sized door with a Yale lock and a double-sized gate with two heavy-duty padlocks next to that.

Ziggy pads over to the hoarding, puts his paw on the door and turns his head to give me a look.

'Yes, I'm impressed,' I say. 'That's some proper tracking there.'

The look turns long-suffering, like my history teacher when he thinks I'm going to ask him a question.

'Thanks,' I say. 'Give mad love to Thistle for me.'

Ziggy nods, turns and walks away.

Once the collie is out of sight, Indigo pops out of a hedge like a ninja and I spot Sugar Niner, Zebra and a couple of foxes I don't recognise skulking in the gardens on either side of the house. Indigo jumps from a wall onto Simon's shoulder. He doesn't seem to notice, let alone mind, the weight.

'Sugar,' says Indigo, 'take a team and check the back for access, put surveillance in place and report back.'

'Roger,' says Sugar Niner, and vanishes into the next-door garden followed by a couple of foxes.

'Zebra,' says Indigo. 'Head back to Lucifer and report.'

'Hold on,' I say.

'Wait one,' Indigo tells Zebra, and then asks if I've got any instructions.

'Ask Lucifer to take the teams off the perimeter and put them around the Tumulus,' I say in my best Nightingale voice. 'Track any Sugars coming out, but intercept any trying to get in.'

'Intercept?' says Zebra in shock.

'We're Charlie Fox,' says Indigo. 'Covert only. Dogs, cats, yes. But we don't do human sanctions.'

'Ow,' says Simon as Indigo inadvertently digs her claws in, and I remember what 'sanction' means in spy talk.

'Don't be tapped,' I say. 'Warn them off. We just need to keep it clear until the Feds arrive.'

'What makes you think they're going to find it?' asks Lucifer.

'Because I'm going to call them and tell them where it is,' I say.

Now, I should have called Nightingale. But, you know what? It never even occurred to me. Instead I pulled my precious emergency burner phone out of my backpack, because the Feds can track your SIM card and the IMEI number that identifies your phone. That's why swapping out your SIM when you want to stay anonymous is a waste of time. The Feds can also identify your voiceprint if you're stupid enough to leave a message, which was why I coached Indigo in what I wanted her to say. She memorised it first time – they're good at remembering stuff, these foxes are. On account of them not being able to write shit down.

I hold the phone up so Indigo, still perched on Simon's shoulder, can leave a message at Holmes Road station, for whom it may concern, as to what they can find at the Tumulus. Then I take the battery from the phone, just to be on the safe side, and tell Indigo to climb down off Simon.

'Do we go in?' asks Simon.

'We should have a look,' I say. 'Make sure it's the right house.'

I push at the small door, because you never know until you try, but it's firmly shut.

'Give us a boost,' I say, and Simon puts his hands around my waist and lifts me until I'm sitting on his shoulder. Like we're acrobats or something. On the other side of the hoarding is the remains of a front garden, flower beds crushed under a muddy yellow skip, and two pallets piled high with concrete blocks and stuff and covered in blue tarpaulin.

Unless you're yearning for another long talk with the Feds, it's not a good idea to be caught being black, young and leering over someone's fence. So I make Simon move to the right so I can hop over and use the skip to climb down.

It's quiet inside and feels abandoned. The skip is empty and there is grass growing up between the gaps in the pallets – it's like nobody has worked here for weeks, maybe months. A steep flight of steps leads up to the front door, but the rest of the house is hidden behind scaffolding and plastic sheeting that covers it all the way down into the basement area.

There's steps down, but if there's a door into a separate basement flat it's been sealed up behind the scaffolding too.

Peter and Nightingale have been teaching me how to sense *vestigia* – the traces that magic and stuff leaves behind it. Not just magic, though. It's like people leave behind traces too – very faint but it builds up. Trouble is, you've got to learn the difference between your certified *vestigia* and the random shit that goes on in your head.

Very random in your case, says Peter. But he can talk.

I'm being quiet and blank like they taught me. But all I'm getting is a whispering sigh, like the wind through trees in winter, like someone being sad on the other side of the library shelves at school.

Indigo jumps over the fence and joins me.

Then Simon opens the small door, the one I thought was locked, and comes into the front garden.

'Are we going inside?' he asks.

'Maybe,' I say, and check the Chubb lock on the back of the small door. The latch bolt is still extended and the strike plate is undamaged, so no way Simon should have been able to push it open.

I know all the names of the parts, because I've been helping Peter learn how to finesse locks with magic. It's still easier to blow the whole lock out. But if you're going to do that, Peter says, why not just use a battering ram like normal police?

I turn the lock so that the latch bolt is fully retracted and click the safety into position so it stays open. Then I close the door and wedge a brick against the bottom so it won't blow open.

I turn and find Indigo and Simon looking at me with the same expression on their faces – which is a neat trick when you think about it.

'What?' I ask.

'Nothing,' they both say at the same time.

'Are we going inside?' asks Simon.

I say that we should have a look first, but that's easier said than done since the front windows are covered and the passageway on the right side is blocked by building materials. The front door is the original, I think, made of dark wood with panels, a brass letterbox and knocker. Above is a stained-glass window in the shape of a peacock's tail.

I ask Indigo whether she can hear anything.

'No,' she says, her ears cocking forward. 'Nothing's moving about inside.'

'Try the door,' I tell Simon, and he grins and trots up the stairs. Me and Indigo follow so he doesn't get carried away.

Simon pushes the door and it opens way too easily. Just like the small door in the hoarding.

I put my hand on his arm to stop him rushing inside.

'We've got to have a look,' he says.

I'm thinking that the door shouldn't be open. But if Jessica, Natali and Goth Girl and all have been traipsing in and out, then it would have to be open – right? And I didn't want to call Nightingale and have him come over and find it's just an empty house.

You always watch scary movies and laugh at the white girls that go inside when they should be hopping a bus to the next postcode. But, real talk – most of the time you're not in a film and the music doesn't go all minor key to clue you in.

So in I go – with Simon and Indigo right behind me.

22

Doing It Like the White Girls Do

Inside is dark and sad.

There's a hallway with stairs going up, doors to the left and, at the far end, a gloomy rectangle leading to probably the kitchen. Or, going by the state of the hall, what's left of the kitchen. The builders obviously started stripping the walls and stopped before they'd finished, 'cause there's layers of wallpaper ripped off to reveal bare brick or older paper.

They left the green tiling just inside the door though – probably not worth looting.

'Anything?' I ask Indigo.

'Nothing,' she says.

'We all stay together,' I say. 'No splitting up.'

'Roger,' says Indigo, and Simon nods.

Through the door is the front room/back room knock-through that Peter says is a sign that you're rich enough to have more rooms than kids. It's bigger and taller even than Simon's house. The double-height windows at either end allow in enough light, despite the plastic sheeting, to reveal it's been stripped, too. Not just the wallpaper – there's a rectangle around a bricked-up fireplace where a mantelpiece has been ripped out. The skirting boards have gone and the plug sockets are pulled out to expose the wiring behind.

'Don't touch the wires,' I say as we walk through the room.

'Why haven't they finished?' asks Simon.

'Who?' asks Indigo.

'The builders,' he says. 'Everything is ready but they've just left it.'

'They could have run out of money,' I say, which is unlikely on account of if you're rich enough to buy a house this far up Hampstead Hill you're not going to be hurting for paper. Something to check, though – afterwards.

Simon stops suddenly and points at the second fireplace, the one that once served the back room, and says, 'Toast – on a fork.'

This one is missing its mantelpiece, too, but still shows green ceramic tiles and a tangle of gas pipes where a heater had once been installed.

'If there was a fire,' he says wistfully.

'We'll see what's in the kitchen, though, won't we?' I say.

Nothing is in the kitchen, not even the cabinet units, although you can see where they'd once been. Wires dangle from the ceiling and spew out of gaps in the wall. The old lino is still in place, marked with clean rectangles outlined with sharp-edged grease stains.

There's a back door and windows, but I can't see out to the garden because of the plastic sheeting.

'Upstairs?' I say.

So up the stairs we are going, but slowly and quietly because something is jarring me. Indigo scampers up to the landing and stops – ears pricking. The treads and risers are bare wood and the white paint of the balusters is chipped and scarred. It's really quiet, like 'too quiet' quiet.

'I'll be right back,' says Simon, and laughs for no reason.

'There's nothing up here,' says Indigo, but we check anyway and find two more big rooms, stripped and cold in the milky light from the windows. A third room that obviously was a bathroom – no en suite, I notice – has white tiles still clinging to the walls in patches, a pile of rubble under the window, and a pair of copper pipes rising out of the floor.

There are two more floors above us – the second storey and the attic conversion.

I look up the stairs and I swear it looks darker.

'This house is empty,' I say. 'They've gone somewhere else.'

'They might have gone through a soft spot,' says Indigo.

'What's a soft spot?' I ask, but I already think I know the answer.

'It's where you can fall through.'

'Fall through to where?'

'We don't know,' says Indigo. 'We never fall through.'

'You're telling me this now?'

'It was just theoretical,' says Indigo, bobbing her head from side to side. 'Something we covered in training. It wasn't something I expected to run into here.'

I'm about to ask exactly where Indigo expected to run into a soft spot exactly, when I realise Simon isn't with us any more. I call his name.

'Up here,' he says from the landing above. 'I've been all the way to the top and it's all empty.'

I look up, and behind Simon it's definitely getting darker and it ain't the sun going behind a cloud.

'Simon!' I shout. 'We are leaving!'

He trots down the stairs and the darkness follows him and suddenly I'm more prang than I was that time I was dangling over the railway tracks at Acland Burghley. Simon reaches me with a look of cheerful incomprehension, and I grab his hand and drag him down the next flight of stairs to the ground floor, Indigo streaking ahead of me towards the front door.

I can feel it at my back as we run down the hall. An engulfing need piling up behind us like a pushy school crowd at dinner-time.

I reach the door and yank at the handle, but it doesn't move.

And then everything is dark and silent.

I see nothing, but I can feel the door at my back. I stretch out my arms in all directions, but all I can feel is the rough texture of bare brick or old wallpaper.

'Simon?' I call. 'Indigo?'

I'm thinking that the door to the front room must be less than a metre to my left, and to the left of the doorway will be the front windows. If I wrap my fist in my rucksack, that and its contents should save my hand when I smash the glass.

People have died trying to break windows with their hands.

Break the window, get out, get help, rescue Indigo and Simon.

Why is it so hard to move?

A light appears down the hallway, a candle flickering in a blue and white tea saucer. It's being held by

Nerd Boy. I recognise his pale face and bad hair.

'Good God,' he says. 'Have you been waiting down here long?' His voice is all wrong, proper posh and old – like he's an elder. 'It's like the blackout in here, isn't it? Still, now you're here we can get on with it.'

23

Three-day Week

It takes more than a power cut to stop a Hampsteadite throwing a dinner party, although God knows how I'm going to get back to Kilburn. Julias has offered to run me home in his Renault, and the thought of that fills me with a strange combination of excitement and disgust, but for the life of me I don't know why. He meets me at the door with a blue and green handmade candle guttering in a saucer and takes my coat.

*

Oh God, how did I let him talk me into coming tonight. This is going to be truly frightful and I didn't have to say yes. But now I'm going to have to sit across the table from Grace and make pleasant conversation. Julias leads me into the recently knocked-through dining room/ lounge lit by candles, where the other guests are eating canapés and drinking lukewarm German white wine. There is Grace now, sidling up with a plate of canapés and how lovely to see you, white or red, and I choose red because at least it might be the right temperature even if it is South African. Grace drifts away to fetch the wine and I'm looking around the room. I see the kids – Jan and Helena – God, they've grown. Jan in particular looks like his father when he was young and Helena is flushed from her first proper glass of wine. More than one glass, I think. I feel I should know the other guests, but their faces are only half familiar and they blur into a tangle of green corduroy, purple shirts and luridly coloured kipper ties.

*

Now I see Charles, splendid in a white linen shirt and a grey-green Nehru jacket, and his smile is like the moon emerging from behind a cloud. He's holding court amongst a circle of laughing young . . . I can't tell if they're men or girls. Oh God, I'm getting old. Soon I'll be knitting socks, rinsing my hair blue and attacking young men in the street.

*

Now we are sitting at the dining-room table, which is really too small for the number of guests, so that we jostle one another's elbows. Charles has pride of place at one end, Julias at the other, as we eat prawn cocktails and steak diane and drink more tepid German white and talk about the miners and Vietnam and the three-day week, and I still can't remember the name of the man on my left or the woman on my right, even as she predicts the fall of Saigon. I am sitting opposite Grace, but thank God she's too busy fussing around the table while wearing an orange and green swirling summer dress to talk to me. All her attention is on the tall saturnine man in the blue silk shirt who says his name is Jerry or maybe Jarahk – it's hard to tell over the gurgling and crunching as the guests tuck into rum babas and Black Forest gateau – and through it all Charles beams and smiles and nods his head and Julias is trying to catch my eye.

*

Julias is leading me downstairs into the newly converted granny flat, which he plans to rent to a granny or, more likely, to a foreign student. Cash under the table, he tells me, so that the taxman doesn't get a whiff. Julias takes my hand as we descend and I think that he's much too old, but I don't know what for. We reach the new bedroom, still smelling of paint and clean linen. He takes me in his arms and draws me towards him until I am close enough to see the individual hairs on his nose and smell the wine on his breath. We stop. He looks puzzled. I feel we should be doing something else, but obviously neither of us knows what. Underneath the high cheekbones, crow's feet and grey eyes I can see a second younger face. He frowns and asks me my name.

Abigail!

I'm shouting 'cause there's a sharp pain in my ankle and Indigo is yelling at me to wake up. I get a confused look at someone running away, and back up the stairs – I think it might have been Nerd Boy.

24

The Granny Flat

I came off my bike once when I was a kid, misjudged a kerb outside my block and went head first over the handlebars. Banged my head bad and when I stood up I thought I was going to pass out. It all went grey and fuzzy and unreal. Like I was in an old TV programme set somewhere far away, like Kazakhstan or something.

That's what I feel like now, but not for long because Indigo bites me on my leg again.

Downstairs . . . We were downstairs in what Julias had called the granny flat.

'Stop that,' I tell Indigo, before she has a chance to bite me again.

Except Julias was Nerd Boy, playing make-believe historical dinner party just a moment ago.

And I was part of it. I was Samantha and I lived in Kilburn and was betraying my best friend Grace by riding her husband. Although I think Julias/Nerd Boy didn't know what riding was – lucky escape, right?

'You saw that, right?' I ask Indigo.

'Saw what?'

'The dinner party,' I say. 'Everyone around a table stuffing their faces.'

'The canteen?' says Indigo. 'Heard it – didn't dare come in. I waited until you came out with that male, the one that was on heat.'

Which is a peak thought I ain't going near.

Except maybe later I'll ask Indigo how she knows – might be handy later, right?

First things first – do we go out the front, the back or up the stairs? Looking around, it's obvious I'm not in the house I first walked into – the one that's been stripped and made ready for the million-quid makeover. This version of the granny flat has orange wallpaper, a yellow modular sofa, a TV the size of a small microwave and posters of white musicians I've never heard of – except the Stones, because my mum likes them. The front end is obviously the living room/bedroom, with a door that leads straight out into the outside area. Through the window I can see a cast-iron spiral staircase leading up to street level. Bright summer sunshine catches the railings at the top.

Through a wide square-edged arch is the dining room and kitchenette, with pale yellow walls and grey and pink cabinets. There's probably a bathroom tucked behind a white door with frosted panes.

Simon is upstairs – we have to grab him on our way out. So I charge up the narrow staircase with Indigo at my heels, but before I can reach the door at the top it opens and three kids start down in my direction.

One is Natali, who obviously couldn't stay away from the house, and the other is a boy who was play-acting as Jan at the dinner party. The third is older, maybe fifteen, with long hair and a Guns N' Roses T-shirt. The stairway is enclosed and less than a metre wide so I scramble back, slip and bump down the steps on my bum. At the bottom I reckon it's fifty–fifty which way they're going to go so I pick left, towards the front of the house, which of course turns out to be where they're heading and I end up with my back against the front door.

But it's cool because the three of them don't even see me. Natali and Not Jan sit down on the sofa while Guns N' Roses reaches down into the gap between it and the wall and extracts a genuine brass-bound glass hookah.*

It's suddenly much darker in the flat, and the sunshine outside the window has been replaced with the dull orange of street lights.

I decide that since the kids are busy fussing over their ganja, I'll have a go at the front door behind me.

It's unopenable. Not locked, but totally fixed. And I'm thinking that this is like a video game when you get to the limits of the level. I've never liked those kind of games – I've always wanted to see what was on the other side of the wall.

I stride back into the living room and grab the hookah. It's got some heft. It also gets the attention of the kids pretending to use it.

'Hey!' says Guns N' Roses. 'That's an antique.'

'Don't mind me,' I say, and swing it at the front window.

I swear it smashes. I feel the impact run up my arms, hear the deep bell sound of breaking glass, see the shards

---

* When I questioned her as to how she came to know what a hookah looked like, Abigail informed me, somewhat tartly, that one appears in the Disney cartoon *Alice in Wonderland*. That, as they say, is me told.

glittering red in the light from the lamp, falling out into the night.

And then it's gone, and the hookah is back where it was. All I have is a tingling numbness in my palms and a fading memory of a breaking window. The kids have gone back to ignoring me.

'That's cool, man,' says Guns N' Roses, and takes a hit from the hookah.

It was totally cold and empty when I picked it up, but now it's like I've got two videos superimposed over each other. One with an empty hookah, and one where it's full and bubbling.

As I back away, the bubbling hookah fades.

I back all the way into the dining room/kitchenette, where Indigo is hiding under a table. I sit down on a chair where I can keep an eye on the kids in the front room. Indigo jumps into my lap and presses her muzzle against my chest – she's trembling. I stroke her behind her ears to calm her down.

I pull my phone from my rucksack, but however hard I mash the power button it won't turn on. When I shake the phone by my ear it makes a rattling sound – I won't be calling for help. Assuming I could get bars in the first place.

'We can't get outside the house,' I say.

'There is nothing outside,' says Indigo.

I look out the kitchen window. Past my reflection I can see a stretch of lawn lit by the lights from the windows above and the silhouette of the wooden stairs that lead down from the ground floor. It looks like it's really real.

'It looks real,' I say.

'Not to me,' says Indigo. 'And I can't hear anything outside – only silence. What if it's Uncle Oboe?'

'Who's Uncle Oboe?'

Indigo trembles harder, so I put my other arm around her.

'We don't know what it is,' she says. 'It's unknown, that's why it's Uncle.'

Uncle for Unknown, more old-style phonetic alphabet.*

'Oboe stands for what?'

'Opposition,' says Indigo. She's stopped trembling but is still pressing into me.

'What does Uncle Oboe do?' I ask.

'Plots, kills foxes, twists things, insinuates and corrupts,' says Indigo.

Which is bare unhelpful and we are definitely going to have a talk about this later, but first we have to get out of here. I get up, carefully put Indigo down, and just to be certain I swing the chair at the kitchen window.

This time, not even the memory of a smash.

Obviously I can't get out of the granny flat. But Natali, Not Jan and Guns N' Roses walked in, so perhaps I can walk out with them. We've done rushing in, and we've done breaking windows, so maybe it's time we finesse this a bit.

'I'm going to see if I can join their group,' I tell Indigo.

---

* I remember this version of the phonetic alphabet very well. It was still in use when I did my National Service. No doubt Thomas used it as well, during the war, and I can only assume that Abigail gained her knowledge of it from him. Where on earth the foxes learnt it, or why they adopted it for their own use, I dare not even speculate.

'But whatever this is, I think it sucks you into the game, right? I need to get close enough to follow them, but not get sucked all the way in. Right?'

There is a pause.

'Right?'

'Roger,' says Indigo. 'So what do you want me to do?'

'You follow me up, and if I don't say the safe word you bite me again.'

I sidle up to the kids, and this time I can actually feel it, a sort of drag, like when the wind is behind you. As I get closer, the room gets darker and starts to smell like the inside of a lift after the local ganja growers have been using it.

'Wagwan, fam,' I say. 'What you saying?'*

*

Helena's mum's lodger is just the coolest. He's got like this Turkish pipe with water in it, and lets us smoke pot providing we suck on some Polos before we go upstairs. My mum smelt it on me once but I told her that it was patchouli oil. Which was half true since Helena's mum's lodger drenches himself in the stuff. And, anyway, never mind the pot. If my mum knew about Helena and me, then she'd really lose her rag. She definitely wouldn't like the idea of me having a something . . . a somebody . . . a girl as a very close friend. Especially now we're sharing digs in Cambridge. Which part of me doesn't understand. But the me that is still Abigail Kamara knows a certified gay couple when I'm play-acting as part of one. Even if whoever is organising this game doesn't seem

* Hello, friends, what are you doing?

to know what lesbians are – or straights, either. That's something to think about. But first I've got to get us upstairs.

'I've got the munchies,' I say. 'Can we get some snacks?'

25

Refugees

I was running for the front door when suddenly some total wasteman attached a bowling ball to my belly button.

*

Julias says that obviously babies are like buses, you wait years in vain for one and then two come along one after another. But at least this one is better behaved than Jan, who was trouble from the first trimester to the last. Jan kicked and squirmed but this one seems content to ride out its gestation quietly. Too quietly, although the doctor says that the heartbeat is strong and consistent and that there is nothing to worry about. Julias isn't worried and Charles is always a comfort.

*

The refugees arrive in the middle of a heavy downpour, in big coats and carrying a meagre collection of cheap suitcases. Julias embraces both the mother and the father in the hallway, tears of relief on his cheeks. Securing their arrival has been his project for the last three weeks, he even went as far as to contact some of his old mates from the Battle of Britain. The children stand with pale shocked faces, sheltering behind their parents. I try to catch their eyes and give them a welcoming smile, but they shrink back. Julias knows either the father or the mother from the war, I can't remember which one. Julias's clutch of the mother goes on notably longer than that of the father. I'm guessing she's the comrade from the war, although Julias has warned me not to use that word around the family.

*

One of the children, the boy I think, is cautiously poking his head out from behind his mother's legs. I squat down, feeling my knees click from the baby weight, and I swear, not for the first time, that this will be our last child. Two is a perfect sufficiency to my mind, whatever either of our mothers may think. I am not some Victorian brood mare to be popping out babies until I shrivel. We prayed for years to have a child, and now we have Jan and soon a brother or sister, and that will be quite enough, thank you very much. The refugee boy has such a round and open face and cornflower-blue eyes with long lashes. I hold out my hand and he approaches cautiously, like a nervous dog. His parents don't seem to be paying him any heed. He sidles closer and solemnly shakes my hand. I ask him his name, and he replies in formal but accented English that his name is Charles and he's very pleased to meet me. When he smiles it really is astonishingly radiant, and I think he must be a great comfort to his family during their time of exile. I ask him if he would like to see his new bedroom and he nods shyly. I keep hold of his hand and lead him up the stairs to where Charles is waiting on the landing. I smile, knowing that Charles will take care of the boy and show him up to the rooms in the attic.

*

I'm standing on the first-floor landing. The bowling ball is gone, as are both of the Charleses, and now the fox that has flattened itself into the wall by my feet is trying to get my attention.

'What now, genius?' hisses Indigo.

'Don't move,' I say, because I'm beginning to get a feel for how this works. Something, which I decide to call the House – capital H – grabs people . . . Not people, because we haven't seen any elders. Grabs *young* people and makes them play out . . . what? Scenes from the past, maybe? It has to be real scenes because they're too fricking boring to be fiction. So, hypothesis – the scenes are triggered when you move into different locations in the house. So, don't move. At least not yet.

I look around slowly. The hallway runs the length of the house, with the staircase doubling back to head for the next floor up. I think I'm back in reality because the walls have been stripped and the electrics ripped out. The three internal doors on the left are missing – beyond them is shadowed space. At the far end is a sash window with the view blocked by dirty white plastic sheeting.

Downstairs I can see the hallway and the front door, the fantail window above a splash of colour in the gloom.

I tell Indigo that I'm going to move slowly down the stairs and she's to watch me go and tell me what she sees and hears.

'Whatever you do,' I say, 'don't follow me.'

'Don't leave me,' she says in a squeaky voice.

'Hold tight, Indigo,' I say. 'I will not leave you in this house.'

Five steps down, the stairs go from bare wood to brown cut pile carpet with black and tan stripes running up and down each side. I freeze and ask Indigo whether she sees anything, but she says no.

Another step down, and the light from the fantail below is dimmer and there is a group of people milling around, only they're featureless transparent shapes like the graphics they use to illustrate mandem* in the computer simulations of building projects.

'Anything?' I ask Indigo.

'There's people,' she says. 'Only sort of faded.'

Interesting, the same view but from further up. If I was moving into a different frame of reference, a different zone, Indigo wouldn't see the change except maybe I'd blur out. So, not like pushing through a curtain. More like activating a recording. Unless Indigo being a fox changes how the rules work. Once I get out of here I'm going to have to deep this. Get into the Folly's library and see what all those dead white wizards have to say. But first I have to get out.

Another step – the fanlight dims but the people get thicker and their movements more realistic, like what you see with motion capture animation. Indigo confirms what I see, and I take another step and then another.

I'm halfway down when the figures resolve into a bunch of kids.

---

* A loan word from Caribbean English. Probably a combination of 'man' and 'them' and used to indicate a group of men or people. 'Galdem' is the equivalent used to describe a group of women or girls.

I recognise Nerd Boy, but the other three I don't know. I wonder if maybe Mr and Mrs Fed had their pictures on their clipboards. Nerd Boy is still in his *Save Our Seas* T-shirt and red canvas shorts, and the others look like they hit Topshop with a limited budget.

Indigo confirms she's seeing the kids now.

Another step and I can hear them talking – it's like watching a school play where everybody is pretending to be elders by making their voice deep, except for one girl who is squeaking.

One more step and I can hear the actual words – or at least some of them. Nerd Boy is still playing Julias with a joke Czech accent, but when the kids playing the Hungarians talk to each other it sounds like made-up noises. Like people trying to sound like they're speaking a foreign language.

'I don't like this,' calls Indigo from the top of the stairs.

I'm six steps from the bottom, so I take the next one in slow motion. As my foot touches the next step, there's a ripple like heat haze and when it passes I can see the clunky wooden coat rack hung with thick woollen coats, scarves and umbrellas. Now Nerd Boy looks like an elder, and way more buff than he is in real life – Julias is bare peng and I can see what I saw in him when I was somebody else earlier.

Confusing, isn't it?

Cautiously I rock more of my weight onto my descending foot . . .

*

The refugees arrive in the middle of a downpour. A man and a woman with a girl in tow. Julias embraces each in turn as if they were long lost family rather than people he knew from the war. I'm so far gone now that I have to feel my way slowly down the stairs – only the child has spotted me. There's something desperately queer about her appearance. She seems oddly deformed, as if she has been squashed down into her present height . . .

26

Girls Can Do Anything

And I rock back onto my back foot – out of the illusion. I go back up slow and steady, watching the refugees become play-acting kids, then shadows and then nothing. I sit down at the top of the stairs and Indigo climbs into my lap.

'What did you see?' I ask her.

'Everyone changed appearance.'

'What about me?'

'You too.'

'Who did I change into?'

'I don't know,' says Indigo. 'You got all fat and your bottom got really wide.'

If I had a bit of string and Indigo was wearing a collar I'd send her down the stairs next to see if she triggers a scene, or whether it's only me. I should probably have crept downstairs myself again to see whether the scene happens the same way twice, but I was too prang to risk it.

'What's the plan?' asks Indigo.

This is an old house and, like I said, these memories are true, because I doubt Natali had a humanities stroke history teacher like Miss Redmayne who loved to teach you one subject by talking about another. In this case, refugees, by looking at case studies from throughout history – including Hungary 1956.

'There are three doors to three rooms,' I say.

'Four doors,' says Indigo.

'Where's number four?'

'Over our heads,' she says, and I stand to check. Real thing – there's a pair of small doors at shoulder height hidden behind a layer of old wallpaper. When they stripped the house, someone pulled enough away to confirm their existence and then left them – a patch of dark wood peeking out of a hole and a rectangular depression outlining their shape. They can't be serving hatches because they're set into an outside wall. I knock on them and get a hollow sound.

'It's a dumb waiter,' I say, and lift Indigo to have a look.

'What's it for?' she asks.

'It's a small lift so people in the kitchen can send food upstairs quickly,' I say.

'I could climb down,' says Indigo. 'So could you – possibly.'

I put Indigo down and try to get my fingers into the seam between the hatches. There's some give, but not enough. I wish I could carry a crowbar in my rucksack, but they're too heavy – and hard to explain in a stop-and-search scenario.

'A trowel,' I tell Indigo. 'Or a screwdriver. And if I get stuck in the shaft we'll be well fucked.'

I have a sudden image of myself being dug out the wall in twenty years' time as an inexplicable cold case. *Obviously she was trapped in the dumb waiter*, the investigator would say, *but where did the fox come from?*

Or would Indigo eat me?

'Leaving out this hatch,' I say, 'there are three doors to three rooms – and rooms are where most good events take place.'

'Why good events?' asks Indigo, which is a good question – why did I say that?

'Never mind that,' I say. 'Events is what the House uses to control us.'

'Controls you,' says Indigo, 'not me.'

'Not you *so far*, fam,' I say. 'Maybe it just hasn't noticed you yet.'

'That's because I possess excellent tradecraft skills,' says Indigo. But she's scared, too. 'If we avoid the rooms, that leaves the stairs. Up or down?'

'Neither,' I say. 'We go out the far window – bypass the rooms and their memories.'

'Can you make the jump down?'

'You forget,' I say. 'In real life there's scaffolding all the way around – what do you think is keeping up the plastic sheeting?'

'Oh, clever,' says Indigo. 'When do we do it?'

'Now,' I say.

*

Papa has brought me the most marvellous present back from America, a model aeroplane all made out of balsa wood. It came in pieces in a box and we spent the morning in the study assembling it piece by piece on Papa's desk. I know it sounds strange, and I do miss him when he is away on business, but missing him just makes me more happy when he returns. It took us all morning to assemble the aeroplane, but when we finish it's still raining. But he says never mind because we can test it in the hallway. The rain is hammering against the windows as Papa shows me how to turn the propeller to wind up the elastic band. I smell the clean linen and tobacco smell of his shirt, and love that he is home with me and Mama again. I tell him that I wished I could fly and he says why shouldn't I? Because you need lessons, I say, but he laughs and says that if I want he can arrange lessons. He has a friend with a flying school. I'm so pleased that I fling my arms around him and kiss him soundly on the cheek. Shall we have a test flight? Papa says, and I hold the little aeroplane up with one hand while I hold the propeller with the other. I can feel that blade pressing against my finger – straining to be free. Gently does it, says Papa, we don't want it to fly too far. But can girls learn to fly? I ask him, and he squeezes my shoulder and says that girls can do anything. I see Charles standing in the door to the study – he's come out to watch, a big smile on his face. I take my finger off the propeller, it spins and I feel the model pull against my other hand. I let go, it drops, then rises and picks up speed, whirring down the hallway. I run after it.

*

'Shit,' I say, even though I'm still all weirdly tingling from the memory of somebody else's happiness. It was Grace when she was my age, and her father's and her joy has worn me out. I was lucky she chased the model plane or I'd still be in there – whatever in there means. I'm back in what I'm calling the 'real ting house', although I'm beginning to think that the hallucinations may be real too. Sort of.

I sit back down against the wall underneath the dumb waiter.

'House has us pinned down,' I say. 'We need to deep this out.'

Indigo climbs back into my lap and looks up at me.

'What do you think the House is?' she asks.

'I think it's a *genius loci*,' I say. 'You get concentrations of magic and it can make things take on a personality.'

And change things around them. There's a whole chapter in one of Kingsley's monographs that claimed that *genii locorum* could change the physical environment. I thought he'd been smoking something, but now I'm not so sure.

'We know all about those,' says Indigo. 'Everything used to be like that – before man gave away all his gifts. It's one of the oldest stories.'

'Tell me, then,' I say, but Indigo pokes her snout into my belly and says she's hungry. I rummage around in my rucksack. I find a Mars bar, which Indigo isn't allowed. but luckily there's a couple of slightly squashed cheese puffs in a cheap plastic sandwich container. I offer one to Indigo, who noms it up in two bites.

'You were going to tell me the story,' I say, but Indigo holds out for the second cheese puff before she'll tell me.

27

How the Foxes Got Their Voices Back

'In the beginning,' says Indigo, 'everything could talk.

'The trees could talk, the dog could talk, the rabbit and the cat, the sky and the river – all could talk. Now, some of the things didn't like to talk. The clouds and the rain and the rivers and the sea all felt that talking was a waste of time and distracted them from their work—'

'What was their work?' I ask.

'Not important,' says Indigo, and continues with the story. 'Some of the things, like the rocks and the mountains and the trees, were indifferent to speech. Yes, it was nice to speak to your neighbours or to hear news and gossip, but was it really important – or even necessary?

'"Our lives are quite full enough," they said.

'Some, like the cat and the raven, liked to talk but only because then they could say cruel things and make others unhappy. Dog and pig liked to talk because then they could boast about how good and clever they were.

'But, of all the things that liked to talk, there were two that loved to talk above all things – the fox and the man. These two would talk all day and all night, about the sun and the stars and the way the wind sang through the branches of the trees. They talked so much that sometimes they would forget to eat or sleep, and the other things in the world started to hide when they heard them coming. Which they could from quite a long way off.

'You've got to understand that in the way back when, man was different – he had fur and claws and proper teeth and a real tail that was just as bushy and luxurious as anything could want.

'But, because they loved to talk to each other, the fox and the man never learnt that trouble was brewing with the other things until it was too late. You see, the problem was that if you can talk to someone, you can argue with them. And if you argue, you can get angry. And if you get angry, you can start fighting. Soon everything was fighting everything else, and nobody had time for eating or mating or cheese puffs or any of the good things in life. Then the cat, who loves to sleep above all things, persuaded everyone to stop fighting and convened a grand parliament of everything to discuss a solution.'

'So talking's good for something,' I say.

'Shush,' says Indigo. 'So they discussed the problem for so long that the sun went off to sleep three times and still they were talking.

'"How can we abandon talking?" said the path through the forest. "It is the one attribute that unifies us all. The mountain is not like the sky, the dog is not like the fish, the sun is not like the moon. But we all share our thoughts."

'"But all you ever do is complain that we are walking on you," said the bear.

'"I, for one," said the cow, "am tired of hearing your thoughts on the subject."

'And so everything in the world argued amongst

themselves – all except the man and the fox, who were over the horizon and practising their sniggering – which they had just invented.

'Finally, as the sun rose from her fourth nap since the parliament began, the fox and the man wandered up and asked what was going on. The cat and the path through the forest told them the purpose of the parliament, and they laughed and sniggered and guffawed, another new invention of theirs, until they realised that everyone else was serious.

'"But you can't be serious," said the man.

'"But we are," said the cat. "And, what's more, we have reached a consensus – for the sake of peace we have decided to give up talking."

'"Fine," said the man. "You chaps give up talking if that's what you want, but fox and I will carry on if that is all the same to you. Right, fox?"

'But fox was troubled, because much as she liked man she also had many other friends as well. She particularly loved the soft earth and the bright moon, and she knew if she kept talking, and they did not, they would grow estranged.

'"I will give up talking," she said. "If that is the consensus."

'But the man refused. For even then man thought himself more important than all the other things of the world. And he glowered at the fox for not siding with him.

'"The parliament of everything wishes this change," said the moon, who was pro tem speaker of the parliament. "And what the parliament decides applies to all things."

'"But," said the cat, who had always coveted man's bushy tail, "perhaps we could come to some arrangement."

'"Yes, yes!" cried all things. "If you want to retain the gift of speech, you must renounce your other gifts."

'Man, even in those days being wise to the ways of the cat, agreed. But only if he could choose to whom he gave his gifts. The cat objected, but everything was wiser back in those days and the cat lost the subsequent motion everything else to one.

'"I give my thick fur coat to the ape and its cousins," said the man. And so he lost his fur save for patches here and there to remind him of his loss. He gave his long claws to the dog, who even now never retracts them in his honour, his teeth to the bear, and – to spite the cat – his beautiful bushy tail to the squirrel.

'"For this insult I will enslave you, you and all your children," said the cat, but those were its last words.

'Finally, man had given away all his gifts except his wisdom, which he gave to the fox.

'"Thank you," said the fox.

'"Don't thank me,' said the man. "I do this so that you and all your kind will know what a mistake you have made."

'Silence closed around the parliament like a noose. But everything hesitated because the ground, upon which everything rests, had a final demand.

'"I, for one, am sick of the sound of everyone talking," said the ground. "If you plan to continue, please raise your mouth as far from me as possible."

'"As you wish," said man, and reared up on his hind legs until he stood upright.

'All the things laughed then, because there stood man – naked and bereft of all his gifts. All the things save the fox, who looked up at the man and saw long slim fingers unencumbered by claws, fingers that could grasp and take and reshape things to suit man's own purposes. And saw eyes alive with a dreadful intelligence unencumbered by wisdom. And fox was suddenly afraid.

'Man looked around from his new high vantage and saw that all the world was spread out about him like a neglected picnic.

'"I propose that man become the master of all things," man said. "Any objections?"

'Man waited but objections came there none.

'"Motion carried," said man.

'And that is why everything that wants to talk has to find a man to talk for them,' says Indigo.

'But the foxes talk,' I say.

'That's because we won our voices back,' says Indigo. 'Can I have the crumbs?'

'So how did you get your talking back?' I ask, and hold the empty container in front of her muzzle.

'That's classified,' she says, and snaffles up all the crumbs.

28

That Cylindrical Flickery Cartoon Toy Thing That I Can't Remember the Name Of

Here is a bit of man's wisdom for you – when you think things can't get worse, they usually do.

Real talk – my dad was born poor into a small village with no health care and no prospects except subsistence farming, and you'd think that was bad enough, until the rebels came murdering, kidnapping and chopping off arms. He escaped, but most of the rest of the village didn't. You never heard about it, because it was just one of thousands of shit things that happened far away and you probably wouldn't have cared about it if you had.

Now, my dad did escape. And eventually there was my mum and Paul and me. But the first half was one shit thing after another – and he was the lucky one, remember. So, knowing this, I shouldn't have been surprised when House came looking for me.

*

It's getting dark again and I'm thinking I've sat here too long listening to fox fairy tales. Indigo is trembling as I grab her and jump up.

'Up or down?' she hisses.

'We haven't tried up yet,' I say, and swing around the banister. But as I put my foot on the first step I see a flicker of light from the landing above. I stop and wait – the light shivers and starts coming down. As it gets closer a shadow forms, a figure holding a candle with the light being the flame at the tip.

It's a boy, a white boy my age. The face is familiar. It might be Simon, but it could be Nerd Boy or Long Hair. Either way, it's radiating happiness in exactly the way a clown doesn't, and going up the stairs suddenly seems like not a very clever idea at all. There's a rectangular shadow in the wall – the door to the front room. I decided to risk it and, still holding Indigo, get off the stairs and head for the doorway.

'Let's hope this is better,' I say and step through into gaslight.

*

The telephone is an extremely curious thing, and looks like a very surprised face with the bells as eyes, the speaking tube as a nose and the maker's plaque a squared-off mouth. Mama refuses to touch it, but Papa is fascinated by the machine and held forth at dinner on how it would revolutionise the practice of business in the Empire. You can always tell that Papa is having a grand vision about the future when he brings up the Empire. The trouble is, the beastly contraption never rings, and today Papa spent the whole morning, once we were back from church, glowering at it. How shall we know it's working? he cries suddenly. Silly Papa, I say, we must make an outgoing call to someone we know.

But it is Sunday, says Mama. It would be scandalous to interrupt another family's Sabbath. Then we must call Ezra, says Papa. Since his Sabbath was yesterday. Then do let us make a call, I say. And how do we do that? asks Papa, so I show him by picking up the listening tube and turning the handle. There is a crackle and the operator on the other end asks what number I require. Papa beams and I am so happy. Hello, operator, I say. Get me Scotland Yard. There are pops and crackles and a strange repetitive trilling sound and a woman with a coarse common accent asks which emergency service I require. Help, I say, I'm being held prisoner. Putting you through to the police, says the operator, but then, curiously, I am lying on the floor with a stinging pain in my cheek and Papa is standing over me with a scowl I have never seen before. Why did you make me do that? he cries, and I squirm away from him. He is so suddenly frightening and not like Papa. He steps towards me with his fist raised but Indiana, bless his little red-headed terrier heart, is barking furiously, bravely putting himself between me and my enraged parent. There is an acrid smell like the outside privy that makes me . . .

*

Gag . . . and I'm scrambling through a connecting door into another room with Indigo at my heels. For a second I think I've escaped the stories, but the room only stays real for a moment before the wallpaper changes and the furniture turns dark and overstuffed. A globe hangs from the ceiling – the gas mantle a soft yellow blaze at its centre. A hand reaches up and pulls the chain and the mantle becomes too bright to look at.

I love my new upright piano delivered by Frederick Reogh this morning, and tuned by an old blind Jew recommended by Henry's funny little friend Ezra. It really does finish the parlour, and I know Henry loves to show my playing off to all his friends. Isabella, he says, I married you for your beauty, your wit – and the happiness you bring when you tickle the ivories. He always uses that term to remind me of his low birth, to test me I think, that I do not hold it against him. As if I would. For he is my rough Henry, who speaks his mind and never withholds his love. I stretch my fingers and hold them over the keys, but something is wrong. I can't remember where they go. I stand and reel back from the piano in a swoon . . .

*

Well, duh . . . Where would you even fit a piano in my flat? And I had a choice way back in year 7 – laptop or a keyboard. And I said laptop. I'm heading for the door back out into the hallway, but suddenly I realise that Indigo isn't with me. I turn around and see her standing in the centre of the room, looking up at something I can't see, and she says – 'Woof!'

*

Sunlight and dust and Henry sweeping his hand around the room and saying that this will be the parlour and we shall have music – as much music as we ever wanted.

*

And I am in the hallway, brushing up against the memory of a girl chasing a model aeroplane while the rain beats on the windows. I slip and I fall and my hand lands on something the right shape and size and I'm scared that it might be too late.

29

Abigail Down the Laundry Chute

I'm back sitting against the wall under the dumb waiter, only now there's no Indigo. I'm still in the real ting house, but I can feel the stories pushing at the edges of my perception. From somewhere below I can hear a grandfather clock ticking in the downstairs hall and posh voices fading in and out on a wireless in the parlour.

But all I can smell is Indigo's wee – interesting.

I know what I've got to do, but I reckon that it's my last chance. And if I cock it up – what then?

I hold the door wedge I picked up in the last room. A bit of hard grey plastic with a black rubber strip along the bottom for grip. Either it's left over from the last owners, or the builders used it while they were stripping the house. The plastic is rough and comforting under my palm – it's sharp enough to get me through the first stage.

Not sharp enough to get me out of the house.

Whatever it is keeping us here wants us happy. I've tried getting angry and lashing out, but it just seemed to redirect those emotions – used them to tighten its grip on my mind. If external doesn't work, then I'm going to have to try what my humanities teacher called 'internalisation'.

And for that I was going to need something much sharper.

I can feel the House's attention move from room to room, floor to floor. It's not looking for me. It knows where I am, it has Simon and Indigo – it can wait. It likes happy. Simon is good at happy. It's not going to let go of Simon without a fight.

Genii locorum can feed off things like emotions – why not happiness?

Why does it want me, then? Nobody ever accused me of being good at happy.

I'm good at making other people unhappy, at least that's how it seems to me. Mrs Georgiou who runs the after-school Latin club sat me down when I asked to join and said that she was worried about letting me attend. She said that she was worried I would get bored and disruptive, and I said, well, don't let me get bored then. And she said that was the problem right there. She said that in the staff room the teachers made bets about whether it was going to be a good Abigail class or a bad Abigail class. They wanted me to join the club in the hope that it would help tire me out.

'So are you going to let me into Latin club?' I asked.

'I have no choice,' said Mrs Georgiou. 'The other teachers said they wouldn't let me in the pub if I didn't.'

That memory cheers me up enough to get me to my feet. I turn and ram the sharp end of the doorstopper into the crack between the leaves of the dumb waiter's doors. Even as I get it open a crack, I can feel House coming for me in the drumming of children's feet as they shout and whoop their way down the stairs. I smack the fat end of the doorstopper with my palm, and there's a cracking sound and a sharp pain in my hand. The noisy children retreat for a moment before coming tumbling back with the swish of kites and kittens and string.

I smack the doorstopper again and the pain drowns out the laughing children and the doors wedge open with a crack that I feel all the way down to my heels. I wrench the doors open, throw my rucksack down the shaft and, before I can change my mind, I dive after it.

It's a tight fit and lined with metal, tin I think. I can feel it sliding past my shoulders. Not a dumb waiter, I realise, a laundry chute – who puts a laundry chute in a private house?

If only it were a couple of centimetres wider – then I'd be swooshing down with an improbably slow-motion explosion chasing me. Instead I'm wriggling and scraping my knuckles on what might be the hatches to the ground floor. By my calc, that'll be right by the front door. I give it a thump, but it's sealed tight – worth a try. My face is getting heavy with blood, and dust goes in my nose and makes me sneeze, once, twice, and then one of those will-it-won't-it sneezes. I can hear clanking and rattling and muffled voices below.

Nearly there.

Suddenly the walls have gone and I fall the last two metres head first – fortunately into laundry.

It's dirty, but it doesn't smell – that's important.

30

The Ghost Kitchen

I'm in a kitchen full of ghosts.

The stuff is all real enough, I've just had a splinter from a big rough wooden table dominating the centre. There's a thing that looks like an Aga's big brother that goes across half the room. The walls are whitewashed and the floor is covered in grey unglazed tile. Black iron skillets and frying pans hang from the walls and there is steam and smoke and shouting.

But the people doing the shouting are ghosts, empty shapes of transparent grey. Sometimes barely there and visible only because the human brain tracks movement better than shapes. It feels like it should be hot in here and full of smells but both are faint, like echoes. Like a daydream of a lost memory.

Like whoever is telling the story never got into the kitchen much.

But there are knives on the table and that's what I was looking for. Because it's only a matter of time before . . .

'Hello, Abigail.'

Charles is standing in the doorway, holding a deformed-looking red terrier with a long snout and pointy ears. Charles is wearing a long pink night-shirt and a nightcap with a floppy point that dangles down by one ear. He looks happy to see me.

'I thought you were coming to visit,' he says.

I've got my back against the kitchen table, but Charles is staying in the doorway as if he don't know whether it's safe or not. Like he don't want to get into a beef with me in case he gets mash up. Which is interesting and also, I'll admit, gives me a bounce. But not enough to make me stupid.

I shift slightly so that the kitchen knives I saw on the table are right behind me. They're ghost knives, but the ghost cooks are still banging pots and stirring shit so I'm hoping Charles's being here means they will be real enough to both of us.

'Is that you, Simon?' I ask.

'Never mind Simon,' says Charles, but the deformed terrier flattens its ears at the sound of my voice.

'Whine,' it says sadly.

'You like Simon 'cause he's happy, innit?' I say. 'What's with the rest of the kids?'

Charles takes a step into the room.

His face is several faces at the same time, not blended but superimposed like a freaky phone app – Snapchat for hive minds. I think I can see a bit of Simon's hair, some of Goth Boy, but behind that another face. Gaunt, pale, big eyes. Younger, like eight or nine.

'It's nice to have friends,' he says.

'So what is it you want with me?' I say. 'Why me?'

'Because you're so full of everything,' says Charles.

'Everything,' I say, feeling behind me for the knife.

'Love, anger, curiosity, passion, stubbornness,' he says. 'You're like a Christmas pudding. You're my second favourite thing.'

Second, I think. Story of my life.

I feel the hilt of the knife beneath my palm and grab it. I hold it out in front of me – point towards Charles. Or the manifestation of the House . . . or maybe something worse? Christmas pudding – what if this house eats kids?

Charles looks at the tip of the knife and then back at me.

'I say,' he says. 'What are you planning to do with that?'

'Something you won't like,' I say, and cut my arm.

Or at least I try to.

There was a girl in my class who used to do this regularly until she got a couple of good rounds of CBT,* and she said to use the upper part of your arm so you don't accidentally slash an artery or sever a tendon.

What she didn't say was how hard it is to actually make your hand press the blade down. In the end I have to look away and slice blindly. There's a line of fire across the top of my arm and I gasp with pain.

When I look, I see there's like a tiny pink line – not even any blood.

But Charles has taken a step back.

The second cut is easier but slightly more painful.

'Why would you do that?' asks Charles, sounding suitably prang – I want him to think I'm wavy.

I raise the knife again and Charles retreats into the narrow corridor they must have knocked out when they

---

* Cognitive Behavioural Therapy – in my day one was told to pull oneself together and, if that failed, thrashed by a prefect. I think the modern approach is better but part of me can't help but be sad that a young person like Abigail has to know about these things.

made the granny flat. There's blood now. I can feel it dripping down my arm and smell it in the air.

I follow him out, thinking that I must be pretty clever to hold myself hostage because Charles starts retreating up the stairs. I follow him step by step until we're halfway up and the knife fades away.

'Let's go and see the Hungarians,' he says.

'Let's not,' I say, and slap myself in the upper arm.

It hurts. It hurts a lot. But there's something about the pain that sort of anchors me in a weird way. Makes me feel more solid. More like me.

Charles's multiple face crumples like he's going to cry, but I slap myself again and he backs up the stairs all the way to the hallway.

Now I'm standing inside the bit of the hallway with the coat rack and the cracked green tiles that I reckon date all the way back. The front door is just behind me, but I can feel the Hungarian refugees pressing at my back. Charles is standing less than a metre in front of me – looking unhappy.

The deformed dog he's holding looks at me with big eyes and says nothing.

I almost hesitate, but I'm at the limit of my heroics and my arm is killing me.

'Sorry,' I say to the deformed dog.

And, yanking the front door open, I run out into the . . .

*

Night. The skip and the piles of builders' materials are shadows on either side. But it's a straight line to the exit, and if the door won't open I'm ready to smash right through it.

It opens. I'm out.

And suddenly face to face with a slightly overstuffed stab vest.

It's Mr Fed from the long, long ago time of last week.

'Hello,' he says. 'Where did you spring from?'

'From the house,' I say. 'But never mind that. You need to take me to a place of safety, preferably Holmes Road nick. And then interview me in the presence of an appropriate adult.'

Surprisingly, he doesn't argue with me but instead leads me over to a clapped-out navy-blue Hyundai parked along the road like an advert for Kwik Fit motors. As we go past a tree I see someone's stuck a flyer to it with MISSING and a picture of a girl I recognise as Jessica, mainly because it's the same picture the Feds showed me that first day. Looks handmade. There's one on the next tree too, and on the next.

Nothing with me on it, you notice.

31

Achieving Best Abigail

I am sitting in the Achieving Best Evidence suite in Holmes Road police station. Simon's mum is glaring at me from one direction and DC Jonquiere is glaring at me from the other. Both of them are convinced that if the current rash of youth mispers isn't directly my fault then I am, at the very least, indirectly responsible. Who knows . . . it might even be true.

'He's inside the house,' I say.

'Nobody is inside that house,' says DC Jonquiere. 'We've searched it.'

'That's the real ting house,' I say, and then I almost add, *Your mispers are trapped in the folds of a tertiary subspace manifold.* But with olds you've got to lead them gently where you want them to go. 'It's a Falcon effect.'

Falcon is the code word the police use when they need to talk about magic but don't want to say it out loud. Peter says most police only know it as meaning 'weird bollocks, bad news, send for the specialists' – him and Nightingale being the specialists. He says as you go up the pay grades, people either know more or have access to certain files.

DC Jonquiere frowns so I'm guessing she knows something.

Simon's mum looks really unhappy, which means I'm right and she knows bare more.

'I'd like to have a private conversation with this young lady,' she says without turning around.

DC Jonquiere hesitates.

'I'm afraid—' she starts, but we never get to find out what she is afraid of because Simon's mum turns on her. Which is a bit of a relief for me – I can tell you.

'Do you like your current job?' Simon's mum asks her. 'Would you like to continue in it?'

DC Jonquiere glances at me over Simon's mum's shoulder and I give her a friendly smile to show it's all right. She's obviously making a rapid risk/benefit assessment, and then decides that I ain't worth her career. She leaves. I'm not sure how I feel about that, but for now I just file her name away for later consideration because Simon's mum has turned back to me. I reckon I've got maybe three sentences to sort her out.

'I know you've looked up Nightingale by now,' I say. 'And Peter Grant and the Folly. So you know magic is real.'

'I know the official position,' she says.

'So you know what a *genius loci* is,' I say, and she nods. 'Well, there's one in that house and it can make pocket dimensions and put stuff in them that it wants to keep.'

'Pocket dimensions?'

'It's probably more complicated than that,' I say. 'So when the Feds search the house, the kids are in there. Only sort of sideways – just out of reach. Do you get me?'

'Why shouldn't I just bring in Nightingale right now?' she asks. 'Surely he's more experienced than you.'

'Because I'm the only one that can get Simon out of

that house. And if Nightingale or Peter find out, they won't let me go back in.'

She's not stupid. She wants to know why it has to be me, so I tell her. She doesn't like the explanation, but she can see the logic the same as I can. House collects children – no adults allowed. She's frowning at me and suddenly I think that maybe we're the same – we both see the world the same way.

'Okay,' she says. 'What do you need from me?'

'You're a spy, right?'

Simon's mum is too cool to give anything away, even when she's sick with worry, which to me just means she's a good spy.

'I'm a civil servant,' she says.

'So you can get information, right?'

'What sort of information?'

'Births, deaths, Land Registry, stuff from old newspapers – that sort of thing.'

'What do you need it for?'

'Rescuing Simon and Indigo,' I say, and remember something Peter always says. You make a plan without intelligence – you might as well not have a plan at all.

Simon's mum snorts – it's almost a laugh.

'Is that it?' she asks.

'No,' I say. 'You've got to get me out of here before Lady Fed calls Nightingale in herself or, worse, my mum.'

'Okay.'

'And I need some stuff,' I say.

'What kind of stuff?'

I tell her and she nods at each point and it's obvious she understands the logic because she doesn't ask rubbish questions. I realise I like her more than I thought, and a little treacherous part of me wishes she was my mum – or at least like an aunty or something.

Yeah, an aunty, the cool aunty – that way, I'd still get to be me and get all the cool stuff.

'You can't tell anyone you're helping me,' I say, and she gives me a funny look like she's annoyed and amused at the same time. 'If Nightingale or Peter find out you helped me get back inside, they'll be seriously vexed.'

'Let me worry about that,' says Simon's mum.

32

Going Equipped

I'm inside Simon's pop-up tent in his back garden, briefing Lucifer. Simon's mum walked me out of Holmes Road and I came here while she got on with her jobs. Lucifer is fidgeting, which is bare wavy for her and a sign that she's not taking Indigo's loss at all well.

'Nobody's come out since I went in, right?'

'Not that we know of,' she says.

According to Simon's mum, some of the kids that had 'returned home' had gone missing again and then turned up again. I reckoned that a lot of the kids, Natali, Jessica, Nerd Boy and the rest, were only being possessed puppets part-time. Or at least part-time until now, because Simon's mum said that Natali was missing again and had been overnight.

'I think we set something off,' I say. 'I think it's getting stronger.'

'You say "we" but you mean "you",' says Lucifer.

'Say it's my fault if it makes you feel better,' I say.

'It definitely does.'

'But I'm going to fix it for cert,' I say. 'I'm going to go in there and get Indigo, Simon and all the kids out.'

'How?' asks Lucifer, and I tell her.

'Is this wise?' she asks.

'How should I know?' I say. 'You guys got all the wisdom.'

*

I have a nap and wake up to find Simon's mum squatting in the doorway of the tent. Sugar Niner is curled up on my legs and Lucifer is pretending to be a cushion by my head. I watch as Simon's mum's eyes slide from one fox to the other, and then to me. I wait for her to say something, but she doesn't. Instead she crooks her finger at me and beckons me out.

It's early evening and the Earth has turned so that half the garden is shadow and Simon's climbing tree is lit up green and gold. I do some stretches while Simon's mum briefs me on the house and its owners. The cuts on my arm ache, worse than when I first made them. My upper arm feels hot, swollen and constricted by the bandages the police doctor put on at Holmes Road.

'They're an eclectic bunch,' says Simon's mum. 'Working backwards – the current owner is an offshore property company acting for Chinese investors. They bought it two years ago from Jan and Helena Dvořák, who inherited it from their parents Julias and Grace Dvořák.'

I remembered being Grace and carrying the bowling ball that must have been one of the kids. There are fragments of somebody else's memories still in my mind.

'He was a pilot in the war – weren't he?' I ask.

'Both of them were pilots,' says Simon's mum. 'That's how they met. She flew for the Air Transport Auxiliary – delivering planes to the front-line squadrons during the

Battle of Britain. There was nearly a TV drama about it in the eighties, but it never got made.'

Somewhere, I thought, in a room in a building by the river, a minion has spent an hour on Google digging that up. Probably not just Google and not just one minion either. I wonder if Simon's mum told them why.

She hands me a plain beige cardboard box with a dozen glass and plastic capsules stored in individual compartments.

'They did take in Hungarian refugees in 1956. An old RAF friend of his who'd returned to Hungary after the war, his wife and their daughter.'

'No son called Charles?' I ask, and start distributing the capsules about my person.

'Just the daughter,' says Simon's mum. 'And be careful with those. They're not jokes and they're quite a bit stronger than what you asked for. They'll be a hazard if you overuse them.'

'How much of a hazard?'

'Don't deploy more than one in an enclosed space if you want to retain a sense of smell,' she says, and goes back to her notes. 'Grace, whose maiden name was Harnal, inherited the house from her father Edward Harnal, who in turn purchased it from one Wilfred Wright, eldest son of Henry Wright, who bought the house in 1870.'

There's a ton more stuff about Henry Wright, who had made a name for himself as one of the new breed of shopkeepers and wholesalers feeding and clothing the expanding urban population.

Hackney boy made good, I think. Married a boujee wife and moved to Hampstead. It's a tale as old as time.

'He bought the house from the Brown family,' says Simon's mum. 'And they appear to have owned the house from the time it was built, which was 1801.'

'Any Charleses?' I ask.

'You asked that before,' she says. 'Is it important?'

'Could be,' I say.

'There's no record of a Charles living in the house that we could find, but they didn't ask personal questions in the census until 1841,' she says. 'I've got people looking through parish records, but their name was Brown.'

At least it wasn't Smith or Jones, I don't say.

She shrugs and hands me a metal pole 30 centimetres long, with a double claw at one end and a horizontal spike at the other. There's a twist grip in the middle – I turn it and the pole extends by another third.

'What's this?'

'It's a hooley bar,'* says Simon's mum. 'Firemen use them. You asked for a crowbar – this is better.'

I give it an experimental swing and then collapse it and stow it in my backpack. She's right. It's definitely better.

Simon's mum hands me a water bottle made from impact-resistant plastic and a round of sandwiches wrapped in silver foil.

'Cheese and pickle,' she says. 'It's all I had time to make.'

We stand facing each other – she doesn't tell me to come back with Simon or not at all. I don't tell her not to worry. She's going to drive to the house and run interference with the Feds. I'm going to go out the garden door

---

* Called a Halligan tool in North America.

so I can sneak over the Heath and hit the house from the back.

'Right,' she says. 'Let's get on with it.'

*

Here's the thing that's causing me grief. I was hoping that Simon's mum would pull out some big fat fact that made the house make sense. There are lots of haunted houses, I've checked out a few myself, but a house with a *genius loci* powerful enough to suck in random teens? If it were just a matter of accumulating stories, then every house built before 1920 would have its own mad god. Peter did a case with a *genius loci* in a bookshop, and his theory about that was it formed because the shop was built into a former cockfighting ring. All that ritualised violence being the equivalent of a Gro-bag in a ganja farm when feeding the supernatural. But Simon's mum found no record of any family annihilation, satanic rituals or any other murder most horrible – and the Victorians loved their horrible murders. If something had happened in the house, there would have been a lurid account of it in the papers.

Kingsley, who was mad keen on this sort of stuff when he wasn't away with the fairies and the water babies, said that such *genii locorum* 'often form around a singular event much like a pearl forms around a single particulate'.

I was missing something but real talk – sometimes you've got to go with what you've got.

*

I'm standing in the back garden of the house. Like a lot

of houses built on hills, the garden is an artificial terrace on a level with the basement floor, with steps up to the kitchen door on the floor above. Not that I can see any of that because it's hidden behind scaffolding and plastic sheeting.

I reckon it's time to phone Nightingale. Not even the Jag will get him here before I can breach the house.

He picks up on the first ring. I was hoping for voice-mail, but Peter's been teaching him bad habits.

'Abigail, where are you?' he asks.

I tell him where and why, but I leave out Simon's mum.

'Abigail,' he says in his most old-fashioned voice, 'I forbid this – it's too dangerous.' I can hear the ambience changing behind his voice.

'It's not going to let you in,' I say. 'It's not going to let any grown-ups in, and you're the oldest old that ever was.'

'At least wait outside until I can join you,' he says – he's outside the Folly now.

But I'm wise in the ways of grown-ups, and I know that once he's here he'll stop me – he has no choice.

I'm tempted to tell him I'll wait, but apart from my brother I think Nightingale is the only person I've never lied to.

'If I'm not out in two hours,' I say, 'start taking the house apart.'

In Nightingale's background I hear the antique clunk of the Jag's door closing, then its engine purring into life.

'Why two hours?' he asks, but I know he's stalling and it's too late because sometimes you've got to do stuff now and worry about the consequences later. Because what I didn't tell him is that I'm worried that House is getting much stronger and that while right now it might be anchored to the bricks and mortar of the real ting house, it might soon be able to move all of itself to somewhere else.

And then nobody is going home.

33

The Bouncing Bed

I am standing on the scaffolding four floors up, looking into what was probably a rear-facing bedroom through one of its two sash windows. It's hot here in the gap between the glass and the polythene sheeting that shrouds the house from view. The air is still and smells of brick dust, old paint and damp plastic. The scaffolding itself is reassuringly solid, with wooden walkways and aluminium ladders between levels. Climbing up was easy, but my problem now is that it stops short of the attic. If my plan is going to work, I need to start at the top.

There are two galdem in the bedroom, one is Natali and one is a thicc white girl with blonde hair that I don't know. They are bouncing up and down and laughing like little kids on a bed. Only there's no bed. The room looks stripped, the electrical sockets ripped out, layers of wallpaper and carpet torn away. I'm looking at the real ting house, but the girls' feet stop half a metre above the bare floorboards.

And they is bouncing as if there's springs under them, or a mattress or a bouncy castle.

If I go inside – which reality will I be in?

From below I hear a sharp high-pitched bark, then two more – that's the prearranged signal that the Feds, or worse, Nightingale, have reached the back garden. I step to one side and, careful to keep my arm clear of any scatter, smash the window with the hooley bar. Then I quickly scrape the top, the left and the right and then clear all the fragments from the bottom. From there it's simple. You just check where you put your hands as you climb in, and ignore the somebody calling your name from the garden below.

I slide across the top of a dressing table that wasn't there before, dragging its blue and purple floral print cover and the oval wooden vanity mirror with me. We all tumble down onto a dusty-smelling rug in green and yellow. I scramble up to find two young white girls standing on the bed and staring at me. Both are dressed in blue and white silk dresses with off-the-shoulder necklines, cinched waists and knee-length skirts. The one with dark hair has a flower pattern embroidered along the hem. Her blonde friend has a leaf pattern picked out in grass green and olive.

'Who are you?' they cry.

I'm in what I reckon is Victorian times. At least it looks like a Dickens adaptation, not Jane Austen. My mum loves Jane Austen, so I've sat through a lot of them and anyway my English teacher is dead keen on putting our set books in historical context, so I know the difference between Regency and Victorian. I bet Ms Sylvestor would be well pleased to know that the classes we spent researching what it was like to be Martha Cratchit were actually coming in useful.

'Who are you?' I ask.

'That's rude,' says the blonde child. 'You should answer the question first.'

'I'm Mary,' says the one I think is Natali. 'And this is Lizzie.'

Lizzie turns on Mary.

'Silly,' she says crossly. 'She should tell us her name first – it's only polite.'

Currently I'm not being sucked into whatever happy childhood memory this is, but I got that sick feeling in my stomach. The one you get when you're balancing high up and don't want to think about what happens if you slip.

Like the gap between the trees where Simon nearly fell.

But I've never been so far into one of these memories/stories/whatever and still been one hundred per cent me. Never had a chance to ask questions.

'Pleased to meet you,' I say. 'My name is Abigail – do you live here?'

The girls nod.

'Our father is Mr John Brown,' says Mary, and beams proudly at me.

Little blonde Lizzie is frowning – she gives me a very sceptical look.

'Why did you come in through the window?' she asks – obviously the brains of the pair.

'I work for the Window Inspector,' I say, and risk a glance at the window I broke to get in. In this reality it's still intact, and beyond it the world is white with snow under a grey sky. No wonder the kids are reduced to bouncing on their bed.

Later, says a voice in my head, there will snowmen and mittens and hot chocolate.

'And your windows look fine to me,' I say. 'Are you the only children that live here?'

'No,' says Mary, 'we have three sisters and one brother.'

'And what are their names?'

'Selina, Henrietta and Phoebe,' says Mary. 'And Charles.'

'Are they here at home with you?' I ask, and both girls solemnly nod their heads.

'Our sisters are downstairs,' says Lizzie. 'Shall we go and see?'

The girls jump off the bed, both landing on the floor with louder thumps than I'd expect from five-year-olds.

I beat them to the door and out into the landing. As I expected, the stairs to the attic are separate from the main staircase and there are two more doors off the landing. I open the first to find another bedroom, and the second to a room decorated in yellow and cream with a wardrobe, washstand, vanity and a purple chaise longue that doesn't match anything else.

'What's this?' I ask the girls as they skip heavily towards me.

'That's Mama's dressing room,' says Mary.

'So where does Charles live?' I ask.

'In the nursery,' says Lizzie. 'Upstairs.'

'Why don't we go visit?' I say, and head back towards the attic stairs.

'We have a parakeet in the drawing room,' says Mary.

'Yes, yes!' cries Lizzie. 'Come and see.'

Mary grabs my left hand and pulls me towards the main staircase. When I resist, Lizzie grabs my right hand. They pull me way too hard for a pair of small kids and I almost topple forward. I dig in my heels, but now the girls have both got their hands around my wrists and are pulling with their suddenly teenaged weight. Natali and her blonde friend are both bigger than me in real life, and I can actually feel the carpet rucking up under my heels. But you don't grow up small, mouthy and mixed race in North London without picking up a few tricks. Like knowing when to stop pulling, turn into your oppo and stamp on their foot. Do it fast enough and you can get your licks in two, three times before they register that their foot ain't working any more.

Natali and her blonde friend, now in their proper street clothes, let go and start shrieking. Natali gives me that weird look of betrayal bullies get when you have the temerity to give them a smack.

'You bitch,' she says.

'It's for your own good,' I say, and make a dash for the attic stairs.

34

Our Lady of Shadows

The stairs to the attic are narrow and dimly lit. There's no window to let in daylight and no lamps to provide light. There was once a cord dangling from the ceiling that's now been tied off with a safety cap. This was probably where the electric light was, but this fades even as I look at it. Down the stairs comes a shadow shaped like a woman in a full-length skirt and puff sleeves. Behind the shadow is Nerd Boy in his latest role as Victorian patriarch. I retreat down the stairs and as I do, whiskers sprout from Nerd Boy's cheeks until he looks like an extra from *Planet of the Apes: The Musical*.

The woman shadow stops and turns back to the serious-looking Victorian gent that Nerd Boy has become. She speaks in low serious tones so that the girls, giggling at the bottom of the stairs, can't hear her. But I can.

'Mr Brown, I'm afraid I can do little to alleviate your boy's condition,' she says. 'I fear in this instance I can be no more use to you than a mundane doctor.'

'Is nothing to be done?' asks Mr Brown, his voice tight.

'We are hampered by our lack of knowledge,' she says. 'It's difficult to treat that which you do not fully understand. That is why our work at the Royal is so important.'

'Work I am pleased to patronise,' says Mr Brown. 'And will continue to do so in earnest. Only could you not at least continue the treatment? It seems to buoy his spirits, if nothing else.'

The shadow lady sighs and puts an insubstantial hand on Mr Brown's shoulder.

'As you wish, John,' she says. 'But please, do not get your hopes up. The best you can do is to love him as strongly as you can, and to show him affection so that no matter what happens, he knows his family is with him.'

Mr Brown draws himself up.

'Of course,' he says. 'He shall want for nothing that is in our gift to give.'

'And now,' says the Shadow Lady with fake cheer, 'I think I hear a trio of naughty mice hiding on the landing.'

She sweeps down the steps and I'm forced to book it down the stairs ahead of her. Out on to the hallway, where Natali and the blonde girl are bouncing up and down like a pair of excited five-year-olds again.

'Magic, magic!' they cry. 'Aunty Isabella, do magic.'

'Magic? Magic?' says the Shadow Lady. 'You must know, children, that there is no such thing.' Then she looks at me – or rather, the shadowy oval that is her head turns in my direction. 'Isn't that so, little spirit?'

'Please, oh, please,' say the girls, while I shiver and press myself against the wall.

The Shadow Lady turns her shadow head back to the girls, who are now much shorter again and back in their pretty Victorian frocks.

'Very well,' says the Shadow Lady, and extends her

hand in a very familiar gesture. I've seen Peter and Nightingale do this hundreds of times when they're conjuring a magic light or levitating something.

The Shadow Lady is doing magic.

Only I don't see anything – no light, no sparkle, no nothing.

The girls do and so does Mr Brown – judging by their wide eyes and the oohs and aahs.

And while they're distracted I make a dash for the attic.

35

The Wooden Hill

I try creeping first but I'm only up the first couple of steps when I hear the Shadow Lady call behind me.

'Little spirit, little spirit, where dost thou wander?'

Elder wrangling for fun and profit – approach number one – pretend you can't hear them. I keep going and she calls again.

'Little spirit?' A sing-song voice like she's telling a story. 'Are you a mischievous spirit?'

Part of me is thinking, ignore and get up the fricking stairs, but another part is thinking, who is this shadow lady who can see me? She's not being played by one of the teens, and however real the story gets, she stays a shadow.

A river goddess once told me that she could tell practitioners from ordinary people because learning how to use magic is like wrapping the power around you like a blanket. Maybe if you do that all your life, then your ghost will do the same thing – holding the power in so it isn't wasted on keeping up appearances.

So is the Shadow Lady the ghost of a practitioner? I thought they were all men, all the portraits in the Folly are men – total trouser fest. Or is it like Miss Redmayne says about science and art and literature – did all the women get photoshopped into oblivion?

And is this something I should be worrying about right now?

'Little spirit,' she calls. 'At least tell me your name.'

I turn and look – big mistake – she's right behind me and like a flash she's grabbed my shoulder.

Her face is still a solid shadow but now I can see smudges of less dark defining eyebrows, the line of her nose – the curve of her mouth as she smiles.

'Aha,' she says. 'Quite solid after all.'

Elder wrangling – approach two – defy expectations.

'I am,' I say. 'But you're like well psychosomatic.'

'That's a long word for such a little spirit,' she says. 'What does it mean?'

'It means because my brain thinks you're real then my body thinks you're touching me,' I say. 'But you ain't.'

Although real thing here – I ain't sure that's strictly true.

'Interesting,' says the Shadow Lady. 'From the Greek – psycho and . . . somatic? From the French *somatique* perhaps. Bad form there, mixing languages like that. Although one could argue, I suppose, that *somatique* is also derived from the Greek.'

'Sorry,' I say. 'Haven't done Greek yet.'

'Oh, but you must study Greek,' says the Shadow Lady, 'Homer, Marcus Aurelius has some wonderful epigrams, and that's not to mention Sappho, of course.' There is a sudden pause and the Shadow Lady cocks her head to one side. 'What were we talking about?'

'Your non-existence,' I say.

'Alleged non-existence,' she says, and gives my shoulder a gentle shake.

'Are you a practitioner?' I ask. 'A wizard?'

'Sorceress, my dear,' she says. 'Practitioner is how the gentlemen have styled themselves, as quacks now style themselves as physicians. How do you know these things, spirit?'

There are things I'm dying to ask but the clock is ticking.

'When were you born?' I ask.

'That's a personal question.'

'Can you remember your birthday?'

'I am a child of May,' says the Shadow Lady, and lets go of my shoulder. 'The first of May in the Year of Our Lord 1782, to be exact. Now you?'

'February,' I say. 'The year 2000.'

'You jest,' she says, and then hesitates. 'No . . . I see that you do not.' She holds up her hand as if to examine it. I wonder what she sees. 'I am a ghost, am I not?'

'Maybe,' I say. 'I don't know – it's complicated.'

'Damn and bother,' she says. 'I must think on this.'

And she's gone.

Just when I was beginning to like her – oh well.

I go up the stairs like a kid, scrambling on hands and feet, and I'm two metres from the top and thinking I might make it when all the energy drains out of me. Suddenly my arms and legs are heavy – it's bare effort to get my feet and hands on the next step. The steps are polished and slippery under my fingers, my neck won't keep my head up, and I'm close to the top but I can't make my right arm lift over the threshold. I slump down and my cheek rests on the smooth wood. I can't remember why I'm supposed to be staying awake.

36

Bedfordshire

I am sitting up in bed next to Charles while Selina, Henrietta and Phoebe are putting on their version of *A Midsummer Night's Dream,* which Mama says owes less to Shakespeare and much more to Thomas Bowdler. Phoebe is a delight as Puck and Selina stamps around in trousers, speaking in a low voice to be Bottom. Papa says that Selina would be happier if she could always wear trousers, but I do not think Mama approves. It's certainly nothing like the play I read at school . . . only I've never been to school. Papa says I'm too sick to be sent away and I've always had tutors since I can remember.

*

Indiana keeps whining and Mama says that it is peculiar because normally she's such a good little dog, but she keeps on jumping onto my knees and looking at me with big eyes that are slotted like a cat's. That strikes me as curious and peculiar, but when I ask Papa he says that God has created animals in infinite variety, including dogs that have eyes like a cat. Charles says my brain is getting too hot. Any hotter, he says, and Nanny could put a kettle on my head for her morning tea. He reads me a story about a boy who lives in a tower with his family, but one day his family leave and he finds himself all alone. I ask him to stop reading because it's such a sad story, but he says I should be patient because it has a happy ending. I snuggle down again and Indiana curls up against my side and Charles finishes the story. The boy, it seems, had a wonderful musical instrument that charmed anyone who heard it, and he took this instrument to the top of the tower and started to play. The music spread all the way to a nearby town, but it was too pure for fathers and mothers to hear – only children could listen. Many of the children were unhappy or dissatisfied, but when they heard the music their hearts were filled with joy. I ask what kind of musical instrument it is and Charles asks me what kind I think it is. Well, obviously, I say, it must be a flute like that of the Pied Piper. No, says Charles quickly, it's a trumpet. It can't be a flute because the sound wouldn't carry all the way to the town. Which I'm not sure makes sense, but it's just a story so I suppose it doesn't have to. Charles says that the boy played his trumpet so sweetly that soon all the good-hearted children of the town had gathered in his tower and they all lived happily ever after – the end.

Is that it? Well, yes – don't you like a happy ending? What did they live on? Pardon? If there wasn't anybody to cook, then what did they have for tea? They had goblin servants who did all the fetching and carrying. And cooking. Yes, but where did the food come from? I think it's time for you to go to sleep now.

*

'Hello, little spirit,' whispers a voice.

I'm lying in a soft, warm bed with an old-style quilt

and blankets and a huge pillow that is leaking down out of its seams. It's the biggest bed I've ever been in, I barely reach halfway to the end where the brass bedstead rises up like the bars of a cage. To my left a boy is sleeping far away on the other side of the bed – all I can see of him is a pink nightcap pulled down onto a shock of black hair.

Between us lies an enormous fox, making strange giggling noises in its sleep.

'Little spirit,' hisses the voice. 'Awake now.'

The Shadow Lady is standing at the end of the bed but I don't want to talk to her. I'm warm and comfortable and want to be sleeping. But this isn't my bed and the white boy in the pink nightcap is not my idea of a good time. The fox? Yeah, well, I was getting used to the foxes.

'This is not your sleep,' says the Shadow Lady. 'This dream belongs to somebody else.'

That wakes me up a bit – enough anyway to remember who I am, but not enough to sit up. I'm still comfortably snug and drowsy.

'It is not the most agreeable of revelations to discover that one has already passed over into the afterlife without realising it,' says the Shadow Lady. 'Even worse is the realisation that one is not even a spirit, but instead a poor shadow of oneself.'

'An echo,' I say.

'Precisely,' says the Shadow Lady. 'And I do not intend to continue in this state for very much longer.'

'What convinced you?' I say, and struggle up until I am half sitting.

'I looked out of the window,' she says. 'Such marvels. I only wish I could partake in them myself but . . .' She opens the fingers of her shadow hand as if letting something go. 'But before I shuffle off, I would like you to satisfy my curiosity in the matter of women.'

My mind is wavy as shit but I see a chance.

'You have to answer my question first,' I say.

'Equitable,' she says. 'Ask your question.'

'You treated Charles,' I say. 'What was wrong with him and what did you do?'

The Shadow Lady sighs.

'The white plague ailed him,' says the Shadow Lady. 'Consumption, that is. As to my treatment – there is a conjecture that the disease is caused by tiny animals, smaller even than a flea, that infest and breed inside the body. Some have speculated that by infusing a patient with magic, one might strengthen the body's resistance to these *animalcula* and encourage a recovery.'

'How did you infuse the magic?'

'I poured it into this bed,' she said. 'I saw no evidence as to its efficacy.'

No, I think, but now we know the spark around which the house grew. Which means I should get out of the bed, but I'm still sleepy and Indiana the dog yawns and snuffles and the pillow is so soft.

'Little spirit,' says the Shadow Lady. 'We had a bargain.'

'Yeah, question,' I say.

'If you are truly from the future, pray tell – what is the condition of women?'

'Better,' I say, and wonder why she won't leave me alone.

'Better in what way?'

Why do people always want to ask you questions when you're tired? I try to remember what Miss Redmayne taught and what they said on that episode of *Horrible Histories*.

'Own property, can vote, get condoms, get paid, same-sex marriage – next year.'

My eyes keep closing, but it seems to me that the Shadow Lady has bowed her head and her shoulders are shaking as if she's crying, but I can't tell why.

I'm tired, the bed is warm. I close my eyes.

*

The girl stands upon a fantastical flying machine made of balsa wood, brass and gutta-percha. She is dressed in a severe grey skirt, a scarlet riding jacket and a top hat with goggles. She has a pistol in her belt, a dagger in her boot and holds a brass telescope to her eye to see the way forward.

Her name is Abigail the Adventuress, the treasure hunter . . .

No.

Abigail the Ghost Hunter, then. Flying to darkest Africa . . .

No. I've been there. Sierra Leone, anyway. Met about a million relatives and only got to go to the beach twice, which was an outrage.

To Paris then . . .

School trip.

The girl stands on the poop deck of a pirate ship, the wind bellying the canvas as her men hoist the Jolly Roger.

Dysentery and anaesthetic-free dentistry – no thanks.

The girl stands on a high branch in the forest, clad in a leopard skin, a longbow across her back and a quiver of arrows at her hip. In the tree next to hers she can see the nest of the legendary phoenix. Within the nest is a clutch of eggs, just one of which will bring her fame and fortune beyond her wildest dreams. All she needs do is jump the piddling gap between the branch on one tree and one on the next. A matter of a few feet . . . One could almost step across it.

Or you could climb down, walk over to the right tree, and climb up that.

But the mother phoenix could return at any moment.

About that – phoenixes have got to be endangered species, right? You can't just tax their eggs like they were chickens. I'm not having this any more – none of these things are real.

I roll out of the bed while, behind me, Charles cries in frustration.

'Stay here. You can be anything!'

But I already am.

37

The Clinic

I am standing in the ghost of a Victorian nursery on the top floor of an old house in Hampstead. Or it might be the memory of a Victorian nursery, or the embodiment of a story about a nursery, or something there isn't a word for – or at least one I haven't found yet. If there is a word, then chances are it's in Latin or Greek, and I think that since I'm probably the first one to encounter this phenomenon this side of the invention of the internet I'm going to be the one that gets to name it. And it's going to be a good name, too.

If I can just get out of here alive.

The nursery has shelves of books and chests full of wooden and pewter toys, but is dominated by a brass bed. The bed is big, but it looked even bigger a few moments ago. It shrank as I left it. But other things haven't changed. Indigo still looks like a dachshund wearing a fur coat and Simon is sitting propped up against the pillows and is staring into space like he's watching TV.

The windows are closed but there's no smell – not even clean linen.

This might work, I think.

Charles is standing at the end of the bed, and this time

I get to see him with all of my brain engaged. White, very pale, nine or ten, with the junior vampire look. His wrists are thin and I bet if I had his pink nightgown off I'd be able to count every rib. He's really not well and I've spent enough time in the Children's Ward to know death when it's sitting patiently in the corner.

He smiles at me and it's bright and radiant and so like Simon's that I'm sure he's stolen it.

'Stay with me,' he says, and walks towards me. 'In the bed where it's nice and warm.'

We're face to face – almost close enough to kiss – which gives me an idea.

'If you like me so much,' I say, 'why don't we have sex?'

Charles takes an actual step backwards, a look of horror on his face.

'Sex?' he says. 'That's dirty. Why?'

'It makes people happy,' I say – and it certainly makes Mum happy, which I know despite her trying to muffle it with a pillow. 'How about a kiss?'

I pucker up and lean forward.

Charles jumps backwards, a disgusted look on his face. That was me when I was nine. All right, truth be told, that was me when I was twelve, too. But since then I'm coming round to the idea – in theory. There may be some experimentation in the future with an appropriate range of test subjects. Once I've worked out what the range is, of course.

'Abigail and Charlie sitting in a tree,' I say, 'K-I-S-S-I-N-G.'

'No,' he says in a voice that is too deep and too old to be that of a poor sod of a boy who's spent most of his short life trapped in the attic. I squint at him and there's a booky kind of solidness about him – a fleeting cement pattern on his nightshirt, flashes of yellow-red brick in his eyes.

'You're not him,' I say. 'Are you?'

'Darling Abigail, always thinking, always looking for answers,' says Charles. 'I'm not poor Charles who was trapped up here in his unreliable body – although certainly I can relate. His memories are part of me, a foundational part, as are those of many of the ones that sheltered under my roof.'

He's been talking but I've been moving slowly. A millimetre at a time towards the stairs, looking to put the bed between me and Charles, who maybe I should be calling House now, and get close enough to make a grab for Simon.

'Although, let's be honest,' says Charles, his voice grown older – less Dickens, more downstairs *Downton*, 'by the standards of the time, young Charles's life was not too awful – now was it?'

'Everyone's life could be better,' I say, but I'm not really concentrating because I'm feeling for the plugs I have stashed in the pocket of my jeans.

'What about your brother?' asks Charles. 'What about his happiness?'

I open my mouth to speak but nothing comes out.

'How long does he have left?'

'What the fuck do you know about anything?' I yell – control gone – fist clenched – why am I so easy to mess with?

Charles speaks again, only now his voice is high-pitched, a girl, familiar. Someone I know.

'It's so sad,' he says. 'She's got like this brother with one of them diseases, you know, like you're born with it. You start off okay but like you get worse and worse and then you die, like, before you're twenty. Like I said, sad, innit?'

Charles has made a mistake. He had to prove himself and that little pause let me pattern myself and get myself under control. I take a big breath and let it out slowly. He thinks he's got a deal. I'm thinking I should find out what it is – because you never know.

It might be a good deal.

'What *about* Paul?'

'He could live here,' says Charles. 'With me – forever.'

'What, as a ghost? No thank you.'

The wizards never really settled whether ghosts were people or not, but I've met enough ghosts and played enough video games with crappy AI to know that, at best, ghosts are bad imitations of people and, at worst – sad memories. The Shadow Lady certainly felt the same. And she should know.

'You misunderstand me, Abigail,' says Charles. 'Here with me outside time – outside death.'

Outside time, outside time, outside time?

Sooner or later there will be a cure, everybody knows that – a retrovirus, a gene replacement or a drug therapy or all of those – but not soon enough, not for my brother, not for Paul.

But outside time?

Then why not open a clinic – stick all the doomed kids in a happy stasis until cures are found.

'How would that work?' I ask, because it would be so good.

'You would bring him here,' says Charles. 'And we would be playmates forever.'

'And Simon?'

The pause gives it away and I know the answer before Charles speaks.

'Simon stays with me too,' he says. 'I need him and, besides, be honest, he's going to be happier here.'

I shut my eyes – it would have been a good clinic.

'Why are you blubbing?' says Charles.

'They're tears of joy,' I say – amazed by how quiet my voice is.

38

The Solo

Sometimes, when you've decided something, it's like the part of your mind that's made the decision is setting things in motion before the rest of your brain has caught up. So when Charles asked what I was sticking up my nose, the slow bit of my brain had to think about the answer.

'They're nose plugs,' I say, pulling a capsule from my other pocket. 'Real talk – genuine SAS issue.'

And then I drop the capsule and stamp on it.

I was expecting more delay, but almost immediately Indigo coughs once, twice and throws up all over the bed. She rears back, vomits again – stretches out and grows a beautiful bushy tail.

'Indigo,' I say. 'To me.' And she jumps into my arms.

Simon's mouth twists into a funny shape.

'Yuck,' he says.

'I did a stink bomb,' I say.

He says something, but with his hands clamped over his face it's too muffled to make out. I lean over and grab him by the arm and drag him out into the hall. I want the stairs, but there's another door and I can't risk leaving someone up here. I push Simon towards the stairs and bang open the door.

Inside is another room with two narrow bedsteads and mean-looking furniture – servants' rooms. Nobody at home, but I crush another capsule – just to be sure.

Simon is waiting for me at the top of the stairs.

'Get down the stairs!' I yell as Charles the House lurches into the hallway behind me.

Simon thumps down the staircase ahead of me, and I drop a third capsule halfway down and stamp on it. But even as I do, I realise it was a mistake. Indigo yaks messily down my side and even with the nose clip I'm feeling bare sick and not in a good way.

Indigo is coughing and spluttering and jumps out of my arms – skipping the last third of the stairs. Behind me there is a wail that starts like a child's but goes all weirdly loud and deep, like something that lives under water and eats whales. I jump the last of the steps.

'You two!' I shout at Simon and Indigo. 'Out the front door!'

Amazingly, they don't argue.

There are three rooms on the second floor, only one has kids in it – Nerd Boy, Long Hair and a girl I don't know. The walls have turned all stripped and peeling – we're back in the real ting house and the kids have two seconds to look about before the smell hits them and they run for the door.

All I have to do is make sure they go down, not up.

'Abigail!' A voice as loud and as deep as a foundation and full of grinding bricks. 'What have you done?'

I want to shout something clever like 'smell you later', but I'm trying not to gag as I half-run, half-slide down the stairs to the first floor. The smell is obviously running ahead of me, because the hallway is full of choking kids. I have to shove one boy in the right direction – he snarls, I shove him again, and he almost falls down the stairs.

Wood splinters above me as if something bare heavy has crashed down onto the staircase. I follow snarling boy down, trying not to think what the spirit of a house might be able to do physically – if it was vexed enough.

On the ground floor they're already trooping out. And, amazingly, Simon is standing by the front door waving them through like a lollipop lady.* I check the knocked-through reception/dining room, the kitchen and toilet under the stairs. But everyone has gone.

I look at the door to the stairs down to the basement flat. I don't want to, but sometimes it's not about what you want, is it?

'Out out out!' I shout at Simon and Indigo. 'I'm right behind you.'

Unfortunately, so is House.

I go down the basement stairs, out into what was once the kitchen and servants' quarters, then a bong-infested granny flat, and then no doubt rented out to – I don't know . . . Who can afford a flat this far up the hill in Hampstead? In the real ting house it was an empty shell, one big room stripped out and with the doors and windows sealed against squatters. Almost totally dark.

'Who's that?'

Natali is standing in the shadows.

'It's me. Abigail,' I say, and crush the last of my capsules underfoot.

'Abigail?' she says.

* School crossing guard.

186

'The happening has been moved to a different venue,' I say, and grab her arm. She resists, but once the smell hits her she's keener than me to get out.

I follow her up the stairs and out into the ground-floor hall. There is a rectangle of daylight ahead, and luckily Natali makes straight for it.

Then it's the 1970s again. Julias is having a dinner party. The daylight has gone. I can feel myself slipping back into the space Grace Dvořák left behind when she died.

'It's not going to work,' I say, even as I remember her first solo, pulling the stick back and feeling the plane rotate under her, the sudden smoothness as the wheels leave the ground and the sudden terrifying sense that she was in sole control of her destiny. And then climbing up, high into a blue sky above the lush apple orchards of Kent.

'But for this gift,' I say, 'I thank you.'

And wrapping Grace's memory around me, I walk out into the light.

39

A Long Delayed But Inevitable Grounding

'm standing outside the house in the twilight with blue lights flashing all around me.

And hordes of Feds are sorting through the posse of teenagers that I, Abigail Kamara, have led from the valley of death – not that I'm going to get any credit. Not even an Amazon voucher.

Simon is sitting in his mum's sensible Audi and waving at me through the window. I wave back, but Simon's mum is standing between me and the car and making it clear that's the way it's going to stay.

Nightingale is doing a one-man sweep of the house. Sensibly, he's wearing breathing apparatus he got from the fire brigade. I don't think I've got much time before he finishes and happens to me big time, so I get straight to the point.

'You've got to let Simon go,' I say to his mum.

'I'll thank you to keep your nose out of my business,' she says.

'I get it, right,' I say. 'I really do, because you love him, I get that. But he's never going to be clever.'

She wants to tell me to shut up and mind my own

business. But she knows she owes me and, more important-ly, she knows I'm right.

'He has difficulties,' she says.

'That are never going to go away,' I say, and she rears back as if I've slapped her –which I'm totally prepared to do if it comes to that. 'In your head you keep hoping that if you just keep encouraging him, he's going to be the boy you dreamed of. But he's never going to be some-thing he isn't.'

'Are we talking about my son?' she says – spitting out the words. 'Or your brother?'

And that hurts. I ain't lying, that hurts – and I feel my face twisting up. But I know that pain she's feeling. I've seen that pain in my mum when she's tired and sad and wants to know, why her? Why did this shit happen to her? And she gets snappy with me and Dad and says things.

'Both,' I say. 'But the difference is Simon has a future – if you let him have it.'

Simon's mum has her mask back on, which is good. Because she's easier to deal with when she's like this.

'And how might I do that?' she asks.

'You want to send him somewhere where he can be free, where there's no pressure. I know there's posh schools that are like that. He likes to run, he likes games and he likes meeting people – he's good at happy,' I say. And for some reason I have to stop and not cry. 'That's rare, isn't it? You should love him for that.'

Now she's not crying too. And we're both concentrat-ing hard because it's a contest and whoever cracks first pays a forfeit.

I win – obviously.

'I'll take it under advisement,' she says.

*

I'm so grounded that Nightingale had to come over to my ends and debrief me in the living room. I thought Mum would want to sit in, but she decided that she'd take the opportunity to take Paul out for a walk. Nightingale helped her get Paul down the stairs and settle him into his wheelchair.

By rights, we should have been allocated a ground-floor flat when Paul stopped being able to walk. But we're still on the waiting list.

Once Mum and Paul are safely gone, Nightingale makes me sit on the sofa and draws up the armchair so he can sit facing me. Nightingale is wearing his own mask. But after dealing with Simon's mum, I'm feeling kind of invincible.

'Now,' says Nightingale. 'Where do you think you first went wrong?'

'Wrong like what?'

His question is confusing me. I was expecting a lecture and I'm sure a lecture is coming. But Nightingale is going all humanities teacher on me. This is not what I expect from him.

'You saw a problem,' he says. 'You investigated, but you allowed yourself to be trapped in the house. Worse, you allowed your friend to be trapped with you. Which necessitated a second rescue mission back into the house.'

'I couldn't leave him in there,' I say.

'Quite so,' he says, and nods. 'But, in the first instance, what was your first mistake?'

'I should have wedged the front door open,' I say. 'Or taken it off its hinges.'

'Before that?'

I sigh, because I know the answer – have known the answer even as I was making that first mistake back when the Feds first showed me the picture.

'I should have told you,' I say, and Nightingale's smile broadens and for a moment he reminds me of Simon.

'And why should you have told me?' he asks.

'Because you're my teacher?'

'But I'm not your teacher,' he said. 'At least not yet.'

'Because you're the Feds,' I say, and I'm beginning to get vexed. I like to get my lectures over and done with so I can get on with my life.

'It's true that the case did fall within the purview of the Folly,' he says. 'But that is not the true reason you should have told me.'

'Then why?' I ask, because otherwise we might be at this all afternoon.

'Because you should never enter a potentially dangerous environment without first establishing reliable lines of communication,' he says. 'Had you done that, you would have saved me a great deal of time. And your parents a great deal of anxiety.'

Sometimes not saying something clever is the clever thing to do.

'Roger that,' I say – thinking fox.

There's a long pause where we both decide whether it's worth saying any more on the subject.

'Have you told Peter?' I ask.

'Would you prefer he didn't know?'

'Yeah, actually,' I say. 'Why? Haven't you told him?'

'Peter has quite enough on his plate at the moment,' says Nightingale. 'And besides, I thought I might use it as leverage to keep you on the straight and narrow.'

He's having a laugh, of course. But part of the trick to managing your elders is making them think they're managing you.

We arrange for him to drop off some books from the Folly library, and he promises to ask my mum if I can go there for lessons. She's probably going to say yes, because the Folly is close to the hospital, and she's bound to need some help with Paul sooner or later. After making me promise, again, that I wasn't going to do anything reckless without telling him first, Nightingale leaves.

I grab a Supermalt from the fridge and sit back down to see what's on Sky.

'Well, that could have been worse,' says Indigo from behind the sofa.

'Bad enough,' I say as she slinks into the space beside me and plonks her head in my lap. I scrunch the soft fur around her neck and she makes little squeaky sounds.

'You didn't see him when he found out that Simon's mother had let you go back in,' says another voice from behind the sofa. 'I thought he was going to terminate the female with extreme prejudice.'

'How many of you are there?' I ask, as Sugar Niner jumps up onto the back rest. 'You better not have made a mess.'

'Real talk, Abi,' says Sugar Niner. 'The air went greasy and the Nightingale blew a hole in the pavement. I was bare prang and no mistake.'

'Believe it, fam,' says Indigo.

40

Ghost Hunter, Fox Whisperer, Troublemaker

I t's a rainy Wednesday morning in November and I'm
standing in front of the house, which is still hidden
behind a wooden construction barrier. Above the level of
the shield I can see that the scaffolding has been replaced
by structural timbers and acrow props. The plastic sheeting, which I've learnt is actually called Monarflex, hangs
in shreds. It looks untidy, old, derelict.

The rain is spattering on the pink umbrella I borrowed
from Great Ormond Street after visiting Paul there. My
mum thinks I headed straight home, but I stayed on the
46 all the way up to Hampstead so I could check on the
house. Sugar Niner, who's leading the surveillance team,
has climbed up onto my shoulder to get out of the rain.
He smells of wet fur and the Chanel No. 5 I think he
stole from my bathroom.

'There's a lot of shouting and swearing,' he says
around a mouthful of the croissant I've brought him.
'They've had to bring in additional structural supports
to hold it up, but the one you identified as probably the
architect doesn't think they can save the house.'

'Charles is vexed,' I say. 'He's bringing it down out of
spite. You're sure no kids have gone in?'

'Not while we're watching, although Lucifer warns he can't justify this operational tempo forever,' says Sugar Niner.

There's a crash from inside the house, followed by shouting and swearing.

'That ain't going to be a problem for much longer,' I say.

'Come look at this,' says Indigo from down the street.

I prise Sugar Niner off my shoulder and he scuttles off into a nearby front garden. I stroll down to where Indigo is looking at a mark in the pavement.

There is a hole in a paving stone the size of my fist, with cracks zigzagging out all around. The edges of the hole are rounded as if they've been worn down or melted, and I can feel the *vestigia* tick-tocking away like a faraway clock.

'Your friend the wizard did that,' says a voice behind me.

I turn and it's Simon's mum walking up the road towards me. She has a huge shaggy German shepherd on one of those leads that attaches to a harness around the dog's chest. She don't look that comfortable holding the lead, so I'm guessing this is not her dog.

Indigo and the other foxes have booked out so fast you'd think they'd be leaving vortices in the air behind them. Which is probably what the dog is for, but I know right away that neither me or Simon's mum are going to mention this.

'How's Simon?' I ask, and not just to throw his mum off her balance.

'Thriving,' she says, and gives me a funny little nod

of acknowledgement. 'That was a good suggestion. I appreciate it.'

She wants something, I think. Things are looking up.

'In fact, I was wondering if you might consider doing some consulting for me,' she says. 'Not too often – nothing that would interfere with your schoolwork.'

'Consulting?'

'There are situations where I think your insight might be useful,' she says.

I ain't lying, 'cause if she's offering what I think she's offering, I get a little thrill. So we'll see.

'What's in it for me?' I ask.

'What you want,' she said, 'I can't give you – nobody can.'

I stay silent. I hate it when people know things they shouldn't know.

'But I can pull strings,' she says. 'Make sure things go smoothly with the red tape around your family. Plus excitement and adventure and really wild things.'

'And what do you get?'

'I get a girl who can go places I can't go, talk to people who won't talk to me and see things I don't even know are there,' she says. 'Someone smart and brave who I can trust.'

'I'm not spying on the Folly for you,' I say.

'That goes without saying.'

'And I want money,' I say, and she's so surprised that it actually shows on her face.

When she asks how much, I tell her what I want and that I want it in a secure trust fund in my name that I get to access when I'm seventeen.

'Why not eighteen?' she asks.

'In case I go to uni early.'

She nods and agrees a basic scale, a little bit too speed-ily . . . making me think I could have gone higher. But I make sure we ain't talking war zones, reh-teh-teh, and we shake hands. I get a good grip and say –

'You swear now on Simon's life and the Union Flag that you're going to be straight with me. Because I ain't going to be your side girl – right?'

She hesitates, which is good 'cause I want her deep-ing what I'm saying.

'I swear on my oath, my office and my son, I will be straight with you,' she says.

So that's how that happened.

And as I walk back over the Heath, Indigo starts humming a tune from some old TV show that I've never heard of. She swears that it's like a classic spy theme, but I reckon I've got to get these foxes something up to date in the way of entertainment.

Acknowledgements

It may take a village to raise a child but it takes a medium-sized industrial park to publish a book on four continents. So, starting with the agents, John Berlyne and Stevie Finegan at Zeno. Then onto my fellow writers Andrew Cartmel and James Swallow for support, editorial advice and occasionally lunch.

Onto production with Katie Espiner (big boss), Emad Akhtar (editor and anecdote provider), Paul Stark (audio-meister), and William O'Mullane (media guru) at Orion, Steve O'Gorman (defiantly freelance copyeditor), and everyone at Subterranean Press.

In the research department we find Kirsty Potter (Northumbria Police Forensic SOCO), Clive Hall (architect), and classicist Penny Goodman from the University of Leeds. Not to mention several hundred people on Twitter who provided emergency research.

Penultimately, there are the people I lean on outrageously to insulate me from the dreadful travails of the world – Anne Hall, Genn McMenemy, Sara Baladi and Andy Ryan.

And finally my son Karifa, for his continued tolerance of my bad habits when writing (not to be confused with my bad writing habits).

Credits

Ben Aaronovitch and Gollancz would like to thank everyone at Orion who worked on the publication of *What Abigail Did That Summer* in the UK.

Editorial
Emad Akhtar
Brendan Durkin

Copy editor
Steve O'Gorman

Proof reader
Jane Howard

Audio
Paul Stark
Amber Bates

Contracts
Anne Goddard
Paul Bulos
Jake Alderson

Design
Lucie Stericker
Tomas Almeida
Joanna Ridley
Nick May

Editorial Management
Charlie Panayiotou
Jane Hughes
Alice Davis

Finance
Jennifer Muchan
Jasdip Nandra
Afeera Ahmed
Elizabeth Beaumont
Sue Baker

Help us make the next generation of readers

We – both author and publisher – hope you enjoyed this book. We believe that you can become a reader at any time in your life, but we'd love your help to give the next generation a head start.

Did you know that 9 per cent of children don't have a book of their own in their home, rising to 13 per cent in disadvantaged families*? We'd like to try to change that by asking you to consider the role you could play in helping to build readers of the future.

We'd love you to think of sharing, borrowing, reading, buying or talking about a book with a child in your life and spreading the love of reading. We want to make sure the next generation continue to have access to books, wherever they come from.

And if you would like to consider donating to charities that help fund literacy projects, find out more at **www.literacytrust.org.uk** and **www.booktrust.org.uk**.

THANK YOU

*As reported by the National Literacy Trust